"How dare you?" she demanded. "How could you think of marrying without love?"

"Because I want you," Sheldon said plainly. "Very badly."

Beverly looked into his eyes as the ache inside her mounted. She was uncomfortably aware of how desperately she wanted his lips against hers. His first kiss had unleashed a hunger she had never before known, yet had not satisfied her desire; instead, she wanted more and more. Her fear, coupled with a mounting passion, made her body tremble uncontrollably...

Second Chance at Love™

PASSION'S FLIGHT

MARILYN
MATHIEU

A JOVE BOOK

First Jove edition published November 1981

First printing

"Second Chance at Love" and the butterfly emblem are trademarks belonging to Jove Publications, Inc.

Printed in the United States of America

Jove books are published by Jove Publications, Inc.,
200 Madison Avenue, New York, NY 10016

For Pete,
with gratitude

chapter 1

IT WAS THE first hour after dawn, and the sun hadn't risen high enough above the tall buildings on Bond Street to reach the chilly dark sidewalk. A mischievous wind played in the deserted street, tossing sheets of newspaper high, making them swirl and flutter before slapping them back onto the pavement. The fickle wind shifted to tease the lone figure walking briskly along the still lamp-lit street. In less than two hours people would be jostling one another on this sidewalk. In the street only taxis would outnumber the impressive array of limousines, Jaguars, and Bentleys.

Beverly enjoyed the quiet morning, but not the cold nip of the early spring wind. She pulled the lapels of her camel-hair coat closer and quickened her pace, wishing she had worn thick tights instead of sheer stockings. The clock at the corner read six thirty. Good; she would have two uninterrupted hours in which to organize her day without distraction from her coworkers—or her boss—possibly the only quiet she'd have all day.

She passed the flower stall just as the owner hoisted the striped awning. She smiled warmly at him, and he handed her a perfect yellow rose. Nodding graciously, she inhaled the fragrant scent along with the crisp morning air. She and the flower man never spoke, but they had a friendship nonetheless, and it was based on this twice-weekly ritual. It had begun last Christmas, a month after she had moved from New York City to begin work with the London firm. One lunch hour he'd handed her a rose—perhaps, Beverly thought, because he had felt sorry for her, a young woman alone on the festive holiday street. Too moved to find words to thank him, she had let her expression speak for her. And ever since, their unspoken communication suited them both perfectly.

Another two doors and she reached her office building, fitted the key into the lock, and pressed hard against the heavy glass door to open it. She was one of the few employees trusted enough to have an outside key, so she could come and go whenever she pleased. In a corporation with such strict security the key was a reflection of the value placed on her work, as well as a high regard for her integrity. Her lips pursed as she thought about organizing the morning's executive meeting. By the time the elevator delivered her to the seventh floor, she had in mind a long list of details to handle. And, after she'd attended to them, all she'd have to contend with were the dozen surprises her boss would come up with just before the meeting.

"Good morning, Miss Milford. Up with the sun as usual, I see." It was Molly McKimm, the night custodian, a cheerful, rosy-cheeked woman of forty.

"There's little enough sun outside for April," Beverly said.

"And I'll be willin' to bet wages you wouldn't feel it or see it anyway, 'cept out your office window!"

Beverly nodded and smiled again. Molly teased her regularly about the long hours she worked. From Bev's first day, Mrs. McKimm had exuded welcome in her thick Irish brogue. She had even tried to imitate Beverly's flat American accent, but only managed to elicit giggles from them both.

She winked at Molly and went quickly along the hall. Passing the secretarial pool, she recalled her early days with the Whitney-Forbes Advertising Agency. She had begun as a secretary five years before, directly out of school, at twenty years of age. She and Larry had not yet married. Life was full of promise. A crease marred her perfect brow as she remembered her late husband. He was so kind and caring—and dead so young! Quickly she forced thoughts of him back into the locked chambers of her heart. Emotions did not belong on the job. Self-discipline had separated her from the hundreds of silly working girls her own age who couldn't even hope to achieve the position she had. At twenty-five Beverly knew how to control her emotions. She'd had a great deal of practice.

In her office she placed the long-stemmed rose in a hand-cut crystal vase on the oak sideboard, filled the tea kettle, and put it on to boil even before hanging up her coat. She stopped at the wall mirror and impatiently tried to tuck truant strands of hair back in position, but it was no use. She unbraided her thick hair and shook it loose to do it over in the tidy, almost severe style she wore in the office. The kettle whistled, and she whirled from the mirror to answer its summons. She selected a breakfast tea from a row of ornate canisters and doused the rich black leaves. While the tea steeped, she selected a china cup and saucer from the assortment above the sink. Each set was different, though equally lovely: tiny rosebuds chain-linked with ferns; blue willows floating on cream-colored porcelain; delicate ivory bordered in real gold. This morning she chose an opalescent gray cup etched with bird's-egg blue, to honor the robin who had perched outside her apartment window that morning. The beauty of these cups seemed to enhance the flavor of the tea.

Beverly knew her attention to detail proved invaluable to her employer. It was a perfect union, because though Sheldon Whitney's genius was indisputable, it wasn't focused. Without someone to follow up on detail, many of his ideas would have been wasted. She slipped off her shoes, warmed her toes in the thick white carpet, and inhaled the aroma wafting from the top of the brimming cup of tea. In a minute she would fix her hair and begin to work. Her day wouldn't end until Mr. Whitney decided to quit, quite possibly not until long after the dinner hour.

Beverly had worked for Sheldon Whitney for nearly six months now. She had transferred from the parent firm in New York, where she had worked closely with Douglas Whitney, Sheldon's father. Sheldon, raised in the States but educated in England, had established the London branch ten years before Beverly had started working. Already it had bypassed the parent firm, much to the delight of both father and son. Sheldon Whitney was a man who got what he wanted, when he wanted it.

Beverly's transfer to London had occurred at an important time for her. She had been on top of the world, certain of a happy future, when Larry was killed in a plane crash one month after their marriage. New York City had become an unbearable reminder of the happiness their marriage had promised. Just when she thought she wouldn't be able to stand another second, Sheldon's secretary had quit unexpectedly, and Douglas, the grand old gentlemen that he was, suggested Beverly to him as a replacement.

With the challenge of adapting to a new environment and learning a new routine at the office, Beverly's unhappiness, her sense of loss, receded. Sheldon Whitney was the perfect boss, and if she weren't deeply absorbed in mourning her husband's death, she might be attracted to him. Most of the other women in the agency apparently were.

He had been kind to her at the beginning. He approved of her orderliness, her disciplined manner. They worked well together, and he often invited her to join him for dinner when they left the office late at night. Always she declined and hurried home to her shared flat in St. James's Place. The invitations had stopped, and his mood turned antagonistic. She assumed his recent shift in temperament stemmed from a wounded ego. So many women chased him; obviously he couldn't stand to be turned down.

She took a solemn sip of her tea. At the sound of her name she jumped to her feet, nearly spilling her drink down the front of her apricot-colored skirt and white tailored blouse. Sheldon Whitney called loudly to her from his office. Pausing only to put down her tea, she picked up her note pad and raced into his office.

He glanced up in time to catch the fire in her eyes before it disappeared. His lips curved in a slight smile. Beverly squirmed under his watchful eye, color rising in her soft, smooth cheeks. "Good morning, Miss Milford. I expected you would be here already."

"Yes, sir. I try to arrive early."

"Promptly at six thirty," he said, enjoying her surprise. "Molly tells me you're always the first one here. I knew you were a devoted employee, but I never suspected that dawn was when you let your hair down."

Beverly flushed deeply and put down her note pad. She pushed futilely at the auburn waves tumbling around her fine-boned oval face, then sighed and gave up the effort for the moment. She stiffened, composing herself once again into the cool, irreproachable secretary. She looked at him through her dark, curly lashes, unaware of the provocativeness of her gaze. He was a handsome man, there was no denying that. He wore his jet-black hair cut short. At the temples there were hints of silver—that were extremely attractive, especially in contrast to his sea-blue eyes and tanned complexion. He stood just over six feet tall, and his frame was lean, muscular. Beverly could imagine the strong lines of his chest, his back.

"Are you flirting with me?" he asked suddenly. The curve of his sensual lip and the tone of his voice implied teasing.

"No, sir. I—I was—"

"Sure you were. Why try to deny it? You were wondering what I would look like without my shirt on."

"No such thing!" she insisted.

"I wasn't complaining."

"But you mustn't think I was—" she began, flustered. "Honestly, Mr. Whitney, my mind is clear of anything as frivolous as flirtation."

"Yes," he said curtly. "I'm certain it is." He returned to a letter in front of him on the desk. "I called you in because I want you to cancel the board meeting. Call each member of the board, and when you've finished ringing them, run home and pack a suitcase."

"A suitcase?" she repeated in surprise.

"Yes. I'm traveling midmorning to Paris, and I need you with me. We leave at eleven o'clock. Can you be ready?"

"I'm sure I can," she told him quickly.

A smile touched his lips. "And as lovely as you look with your hair tangled around your pretty face, please do something with it, or I'll find it impossible not to carry you off to my apartment and devour you for breakfast."

She was certain he was teasing. He never spoke to her this informally. It must be the hour of the day. Why would he even kid her about romance when he could have any girl he wanted? Surely he found her quiet nature and humble manner, if acceptable on the job, too bland for his rich diet. She studied his expression but couldn't really read it. It was true that his job demanded a lot of travel and that sometimes he took an assistant, but he had never insisted on her accompanying him. There were dozens of girls in the firm who would trade their weekly salary for a chance to travel alone with their charismatic boss.

"Mr. Whitney," she ventured. "Are you serious?"

"About devouring you for breakfast?" His eyes twinkled mischievously.

"About going to Paris?"

"Absolutely," he confirmed. "April in Paris. What could be nicer?"

"Yes, sir. If you say so."

"Miss Milford, what I like most about you is your original turn of phrase . . . not to mention your stockinged feet."

Beverly reddened again before excusing herself. Increasingly she had trouble understanding him, and she was beginning to think he enjoyed her perplexity. His moods shifted from teasing to indifference, from scorn to approval, more quickly than Beverly could transcribe memos.

She ran a comb through her hair, then braided it tightly before pinning it atop her head. She phoned the secretary of each member of the board of directors. They were used to Whitney's sudden cancellations, and although they didn't like it, they knew it was his spontaneity that made the London branch of Whitney-Forbes one of the most powerful advertising agencies in the world.

Beverly had taken the liberty of ringing the secretaries at home. Each one understood how demanding it was to work for Sheldon, and they all wished to change places with her, especially today. She too would have liked to trade places with any one of them. She tried to sound enthusiastic about the trip to Paris, but in her heart she was dreading it.

She straightened her desk and filed away the stack of letters in her top drawer. These papers were meant for her eyes only until matters were settled. Checking her calendar for appointments that must be canceled, she scribbled notes to the secretary who would replace her while she was away. She emptied the last drops of tea into the sink before rinsing and drying the cup.

As she was drying her hands Mr. Whitney entered her office. Good Lord! Everything was topsy-turvy this morning! He never came to her. He buzzed or shouted when he wanted her for something. Beverly watched him closely as he surveyed her office.

After a minute he turned to her as if seeing her for the first time, caught her eye, and held it without speaking. He ran his hand through his thick hair, a bemused look on his face. "Still here?"

"I was just leaving," she assured him.

"I see. Stopping for a minute to straighten up your office?" Beverly nodded. "Did you ring the board members?" Again she nodded. "Were they furious?"

"Not at all. They understand your—"

"My what? My erratic behavior?" He stopped in front of the oak sideboard to inspect the rose. He looked up inquisitively, waiting for her to speak.

"To be honest, sir, yes. I would have tempered your adjective and called you spontaneous, however. But of course they understood, all of them. They look forward to seeing you when you return."

"And what about you, Miss Milford?"

"Sir?"

"Do you understand my 'spontaneity'?"

"I have to admit, sir, you do puzzle me sometimes."

"Good." His eyes flickered dangerously. "Then we're even!"

Beverly stared at him blankly. She moistened her dry lips with the tip of her tongue, only to find his eyes shifting to her mouth. "If there isn't anything else you need, I'll dash home now," she managed politely, anxious to get away from him. Despite her firm resolution, she found herself physically aware of him, wondering what his muscular arms would feel like in a close embrace, how his mouth might move on hers. . . . The near-fantasy exasperated her, and she strengthened her resolve to keep tight control over such wayward thoughts.

"There's another matter pending," he said. "I was going to take Miss Sexton with me on this trip." He watched Beverly closely for a reaction. Miss Sexton, she knew, was the personal secretary of one of the executives in the Agency and she was just the kind of woman Mr. Whitney reputedly enjoyed: elegant, sophisticated, glamorous—and always ready for a new adventure. Beverly fought the outrage building inside her and forced herself not to care about his silly affairs. "But now I find the business sufficiently complicated that I will need your assistance," he continued, seeming to enjoy the moment.

So that was it! He had planned to combine work with pleasure, and now he had to leave his plaything behind. Why couldn't he spare her the details? Why did he find it necessary to flaunt his affairs?

"Since your presence is required," he resumed, "Miss Sexton can take over here in your office. Of course you shall have to arrange for a second hotel room. Unless you would like to save the company additional expense and room with me."

Beverly's eyes darkened in anger. She'd show him! "I'll ask Miss Sexton to ring for an additional reservation, if you haven't any objections," she said in a calm, sweet tone. "That way I can kill two birds with one stone." He was watching her intently. "I'll need every minute if we're to leave at eleven. And Miss Sexton will be so relieved, I know, to learn I am not replacing her entirely."

Sheldon laughed. "So the kitten does have claws! By all means tell Lizzie to phone for a reservation. I wouldn't want you to miss the chance to kill any birds." He had crossed the room and was standing dangerously close. Beverly could smell his after-shave lotion, and it made her head spin. "Doesn't anything destroy your cool, Miss Milford?" he asked suddenly. His lips hardened into a thin line.

"I try not to let anything interfere with my work," she answered, more than a little unnerved. She took a step backward, but he caught her by the hand and pulled her close to him. She did her best to resist, but his grip was strong. "Please," she begged. "Let me go."

"Is that what you want? I think you enjoy being held. Or are you afraid your boyfriend will find out and get angry? Haven't you enough affection for us both?"

"No," she began. "I haven't—" She started to explain, but he was in no mood for explanations. She looked up at him beseechingly. He stopped any thought of a protest with a hard, penetrating kiss. She tried to pull away but was helpless against his strength. She felt his muscular arms encircle her small waist, and her heart resounded so loudly beneath her breast she was sure he could hear it.

His kiss worked magic. Beverly felt her resistance melt; her body seemed to dissolve into his. All her life she had dreamed of being kissed like this, but she had never dared to imagine it could actually happen. And with Sheldon Whitney! Why, he could have any woman he wanted . . . and he did. His reputation certainly didn't end with his business accomplishments. And now, lost in the strength of his arms, she understood why women so willingly yielded themselves to him. She had sworn to be immune to his charms. But how could she be immune when his mouth left hers and caressed the curve of her neck, teasing her, exciting her? She had thought her feelings were dead, but he was proving her wrong. To be loved by Sheldon . . .

Loved by Sheldon? Her resistance flooded back. She was

crazy to think he would confine his lovemaking to her alone. He would laugh at her if he suspected her thoughts had included love. He might pretend love, if that was necessary, but he would never fall for her. How clear all that was! Hadn't she seen—day after day in the office—how fickle his affections were? He concentrated on acquiring a woman until he had her, then he forgot her. Beverly vowed she wouldn't become one of his trophies. She wouldn't risk falling in love with a man who thought sex was the most important part of love. No, she had loved once, and she wasn't going to mock the memory of that love with a casual affair.

Sheldon must have felt her renewed, silent protest, because his kiss deepened, his arms held her even tighter.

Beverly snapped her head back. "Please . . . let me go," she pleaded, suddenly aware of the spectacle she had made of herself. She pushed against his chest, struggling to break free from his powerful arms, but he refused to release her. Her embarrassment turned to anger. "Let go of me!" she cried furiously. And, suddenly, he did. "If you're finished," she said coldly, catching her breath, "I think I should go now."

"You never give in, do you, Bev?" he asked quietly.

"I do my best to behave professionally," she said evenly.

Sheldon looked as if he was about to speak, but instead he merely dismissed her with a vague wave of his hand. Apparently his interest had already died.

She quickly collected her purse and coat as he moved to leave. At the door he stopped her. "Miss Milford?" She looked at him uneasily. "You'll need to pack evening clothes. We'll be meeting with André Couteau. He's interested in having our firm represent his fall line." She had heard that Couteau, one of Paris's most respected designers, was planning to export a line of ready-to-wear clothes.

"Certainly, sir. I'll do my best not to embarrass you."

"I'd appreciate that." He paused, looking thoughtful. "And Miss Milford?"

"Yes?"

"Do stop calling me 'sir'!"

"Of course, Mr. Whitney." She waited for further instructions, but he had apparently finished. He stared hard at her for long seconds, then wheeled and strode briskly back to his office.

Beverly reached the sidewalk in minutes. The cool morning air took the heat from her cheeks, helped to clear her mind. And yet her thoughts were racing a mile a minute. She raised her arm to hail a cab, but the doorman stopped her. He directed her to a limousine—waiting for her, she was told, at Mr. Whitney's instruction.

The ride calmed her, and even the four flights of stairs to her flat calmed her today. She could blame her shortness of breath and quickened pulse on that climb and keep her roommate, Jancie, in the dark about her emotional turmoil over Sheldon Whitney and the trip with him to Paris.

Jancie was curled up on the sofa in the tidy front room, her head bowed over the morning paper, a cup of coffee at her elbow. Beverly watched her for several seconds, wishing herself capable of tuning people out like that. Jancie flipped the page, then looked up absently, smiling as she discovered her friend's presence.

"Oh, hello," she greeted warmly. "What are you doing home? Goodness, you look positively undone. Is anything the matter?"

"I'm scared to death! I have to be on a *plane* at eleven o'clock!"

"For where?"

"France. On business."

"Alone?"

"Unfortunately not. I am assisting Mr. Whitney."

"I see!" A knowing grin curved Jancie's lips. "Now I understand why you're flustered. Really, you look like you've been chased through Hyde Park by Prince Charles." She laughed, and Beverly pretended surprise at Jancie's blasphemy against her beloved member of the royal family.

"You're imagining things, honestly. You know how I feel about flying. Otherwise I'd be thrilled at the thought of Paris. If it weren't such important business, I wouldn't have to go."

"But of course!"

"What are you smirking about?" Beverly demanded. No one was acting normally today!

"If only you could *see* your face. It's alive with fire."

Beverly's hand flew to her cheek. "The wind is fierce," she explained earnestly.

"I had best keep indoors then, hadn't I?" Jancie smiled broadly. "On second thought, if the wind is the cause of your looks, I'll rush right out. Honestly, you look like you've been making love to a Greek god!"

Beverly was horrified. "I've done nothing of the sort!" she protested loudly. She began to pace the room nervously. "I must pack now, and I haven't a clue what to take. Mr. Whitney suggested evening clothes, which presents a problem. I only have one gown I can dare be seen in."

"Why not borrow my new red dress? And you can take the blue one I got last month. I'm not going anywhere, and both of them are *perfect* for this time of year!"

"Do you think they would fit?" Beverly asked hopefully.

"Sure. Just adjust the straps. There's hardly anything to those gowns, anyway."

"You're an absolute angel," Beverly announced, darting over to kiss her friend on the cheek.

Jancie grinned. "Come on, I'll help you pack. I don't have to be at work until noon." She was the receptionist for Beddard's, a noted clothing manufacturer. When the mornings were booked with fashion shows, she arrived in midday and worked through dinner. It was at late-night dinners that Beverly and Jancie found time to catch up on each other's lives.

"I wonder what the weather will be like?" Beverly said.

"Perfect, no doubt. Think I might fit inside your suitcase? I'll hardly take any room."

"Believe me, I wish you could," Beverly said.

When she had first moved to London, Beverly had found a perfect two-bedroom flat in a respectable neighborhood. Although her salary was generous, the rent was more than she could manage alone, and she searched for someone with whom she could share the roomy apartment. Jancie was the first person to answer the ad in *The Times*, and they had taken to each other from the start.

Their apartment was part of a four-story house, and the girls shared the top floor. An ancient bent elm softened the urban view directly outside their living-room window, lending a country feeling to the house. There was plenty of room for privacy, and on those occasions when they were both home and awake they enjoyed each other's company. Beverly's only complaint was with Jancie's social life. She was forever introducing Bev to an "available" new man. Beverly was always polite—and she did like Jancie's friends—but after a long day at work she wanted only to come home to quiet.

"How long will you be gone?" Jancie asked.

Beverly shrugged. "A week, maybe? I forgot to ask, I was so startled to be told I was going." Her face flushed crimson as she recalled her "conversation" with her employer.

Jancie studied her expression. "Are you sure you're all right?"

"Positive! What are your plans for the week?" she asked, changing the subject.

"Julian is coming 'round for supper tomorrow night."

"Julian? Aren't you seeing an awful lot of him?"

"We've all got to settle down some time."

"Really?" Beverly was intensely interested. "Is he serious?"

"He hasn't professed love on bended knees, if that's what you mean. But he sure stirs a fire in me," she added confidentially. "He's not as striking as Sheldon Whitney, I'm afraid, but he is a dear."

"Why bring Sheldon Whitney into this?" Beverly asked defensively. She had thought of little else but him since arriving home, but she believed she had masked her preoccupation. She and Jancie shared confidences, but she had no intention of divulging what had happened or, more importantly, the surge of emotion she had experienced when Sheldon kissed her.

"I was just comparing our weeks, that's all. No reason to get bent out of shape. Here I am, having a quiet dinner with mild-mannered Julian, and you are off for a romantic week in Paris with the King of Passion."

"This trip is business. Period. Mr. Whitney has his fine points, I'm willing to admit, but he has no interest in me, and I have even less interest in him!" Beverly said hotly. "And even if I did, there's no chance on earth that I would tangle in his playboy web. He's a confirmed philanderer. Half the women in London know the inside of his apartment intimately. You should hear the rumors!"

"Hmmm, I'll bet. I wonder if they're true? But you keep your eyes open, even if you are convinced of his indifference. You may be blind to his charms, but he's got his eye on you, and you can bet it isn't half shut. I'd wager money on his ability to prove you wrong."

"My eyes are open. Don't you worry, I have no intention of losing sight of my position, either as his secretary or as Larry's widow. Are you going to help me pack, or not?"

she asked suddenly, glancing anxiously at her watch. "I have to be at the airport in an hour." Her hand flew to her forehead. "If I can manage the flight across the English Channel, I can handle *anything*. Keep your fingers crossed that we haven't any strong winds."

chapter 2

IF SHE WERE making this trip on her own, Beverly would have hired a taxi to Paddington Station in the heart of the city, where trains regularly took travelers to the airport, some forty minutes south of London. But the chauffeur who had driven her home had insisted on waiting.

"Company orders," he explained, smiling discreetly.

That could mean one thing only: Sheldon Whitney. Apparently he intended to make her life as comfortable as possible—while he made it absolutely impossible! In the last month he had been resolutely impatient with her one minute—in fact, almost rude—then leaning over backward to accommodate her the next. As far as Beverly could tell, she was doing nothing different from day to day, or, for that matter, nothing different from the months before, when her work had consistently produced compliments from her boss. Why the sudden change? Beverly found much of her time spent thinking about his moods, going over his words, looking for clues. In fact, he rarely left her mind, even in the hours after work. Was he intentionally disrupting her thoughts? Surely not. He had important things to do . . . and what was that nonsense about her boyfriend? More than likely he wasn't even aware of the switch in his temperament. Just a part of his unpredictable nature. She wasn't in any position to point out the inconsistency; she could merely endure it and hope it didn't interfere too much with her work. She figured that whatever business problem was nagging at him would resolve itself soon, and then he would return to his amiable self. She hoped it would happen soon. Her nerves were constantly frayed when he was around these days.

Beverly snapped out of her reverie when the chauffeur pulled up in front of double iron gates to confer with a guard. She hadn't given a thought to the fact that, of course, they would be picking up Sheldon Whitney. The silver Rolls-Royce passed into a winding, secluded driveway. Both sides of the drive were manicured; evergreens clipped in imaginative shapes grew no higher than the car window. Behind the ornate hedges were fruit trees with the first hint of blossom. Beyond these delicate trees was thick forest, yet even there it was clear that every inch was attended full-time by an experienced crew of grounds keepers.

The sight of the house stole her attention from the grounds. It was enormous! And right in the heart of London! She hadn't suspected that anything so grand still existed within the city limits. She must have gasped audibly, for the driver nodded in agreement.

"It's quite the place, ain't it, ma'am?" he said proudly.

Beverly couldn't tear her gaze away from the impressive sight. "It's magnificent! But does he live here all alone? Surely it's too big for just one," she thought aloud. "Such a lovely house must long for a lot of people to admire its beauty."

The chauffeur chuckled gently. "If you don't mind my saying so, I think this old house is filled up pretty much of the time." His eyes flickered with delight until he noticed her embarrassed face in the rearview mirror. He tactfully changed the subject. "You must enjoy working for such a man. He has all the successes, don't he?"

Beverly nodded numbly. Her thoughts were with the women who frequented the Whitney mansion. Even the driver was aware of Sheldon's love life! She straightened her back against the rich leather upholstery, determined never to be one of his "successes." The car rolled to a halt in front of the intricately carved doors. Should she go inside to fetch him or let him come to her? Sheldon appeared at the door, settling her question.

He was followed by two servants, each with a suitcase. He had changed from the formal navy blue double-breasted suit he had worn that morning into a pair of almond-colored trousers, cut narrowly at the waist, and a chocolate-brown sports coat. Both accentuated his dark complexion and made his handsome face and figure hard to ignore.

Beverly wished she had changed her clothes for travel. She had simply added a spicy-orange blazer over her skirt and blouse. As always, her hair was tied up off her neck. Only an occasional tendril escaped, curling down her long, slender neck, to detract from the picture of perfect order, complete respectability. Not the usual travel companion for the King of Passion, she thought, adopting Jancie's title for the playboy who was her boss. She wouldn't put up with another ounce of his nonsense. She would inform him from the start that she wasn't interested. She was his employee. And Larry's widow. Before they reached the plane, she would correct any false impressions he might have about her availability as anything other than a secretary.

The driver opened the door for him, and he slid in beside her. He greeted her with more reserve than he had exercised when they first met. He was distant, dignified, as if he had never held her in his arms, as if his lips had never burned against hers. She waited for an opening to deliver her prepared speech, but the opportunity never came. Perhaps it wasn't necessary after all. Perhaps he had understood in the office that she wasn't his type. If so, he deserved more credit than she had given him. She glanced sideways for an indication of his mood, but his head was turned away from her, and all she could see was his black hair touching the collar of his shirt. She thought ahead to the flight, determined to conceal her desperate fear. She would reveal nothing of her real self, in no way allow herself to be vulnerable.

They rode the distance to the airport in silence. The second time she dared to look his way, she discovered him staring at her, a lazy smile on his lips.

The chauffeur took the luggage and went ahead to check the reservations. Beverly and Sheldon went into the terminal in a leisurely way, but she was too tense to speak to him. She let out an audible sigh.

"Are you all right, Miss Milford?" he asked.

Beverly was struck by the concern in his voice. "Yes," she told him quickly. "I'm just a little nervous about the flight. I like having both feet on the ground." She tried to disguise the fear in her voice with laughter.

"No need to worry," he assured her. "I'll take care of you." He took her small hand, but that only increased her anxiety. "I cross the English Channel regularly," he explained to her, keeping her hand in his. "At worst the flight can be bumpy, depending on the air currents. But there is no need to worry," he repeated. "You'll wonder why you ever had a single fear. Come," he said, "they're announcing our flight."

Beverly followed him numbly across the terminal. Why was he taking so much trouble with her, she wondered. His words had temporarily quieted her fear of flying, but they had added a new danger: intimacy. Did he think his concern would win her affections? Did he expect her to repay his comfort with her favors? She must not be taken in. Hadn't he kissed her that very morning? Wasn't that proof that he wanted her? He would do anything, she knew, to have what he wanted. She mustn't drop her guard for even one moment, she thought as they neared the boarding gate. She wished she could erase the memory of his kiss from both their minds.

Sheldon steered her past a long line of passengers through the entrance marked "first class." The stewardess greeted him by name. He stopped to talk with the tall, dark beauty just inside the gate. Beverly wondered if any woman could resist Sheldon's charms.

"A lovely girl, don't you think?" he said when they were beyond hearing. Beverly nodded indifferently, trying to cover her real feelings. "You could take lessons from her, Bev," Sheldon teased, using her nickname for the second time that morning. "She's not afraid to fly."

Beverly's face burned. How dare he treat such an important issue lightly. How dare he compare her to that woman! "Perhaps she has no reason to be afraid. Looks like she's been flying all her life," she said scornfully.

Sheldon laughed outright. "Beverly, I do believe you're jealous. I always suspected passion beneath that cool facade."

"Jealous of what?"

Sheldon's eyes darkened, his mouth tightened.

"If you mean the shameless way you looked at her," Beverly said boldly, "or the shameless way she flirted with you, you couldn't be more wrong. I value my affections too much to give them away casually."

"One at a time, that's you, isn't it, Bev? Keep all your fire for your British boyfriend?"

What was this repeated reference to a boyfriend? Should she correct him? She had never said anything to promote his false impression, but as long as he thought she was taken he might be satisfied to leave her alone. She gave her ticket to the stewardess at the door and slipped into the window seat beside Sheldon.

Beverly noticed that she and Sheldon were the only passengers in the first-class cabin, but that the rear of the plane was full. She listened intently to the stewardess's instructions, first in English, then in French, explaining emergency procedures. She absorbed every word, certain she would need this information before the flight was over, but Sheldon flipped through his date book absently, making notes in his bold, elegant script.

She closed her eyes as the plane left the ground; her heart pounded in her throat all during takeoff. As the plane climbed into the sky, she was sure she would die. She yearned for Larry, his gentle laughter, his constant reassurance. She thought back to the blissful month of their marriage, then recalled with renewed pain the phone call that had brought news of the plane crash, his sudden death. She hadn't believed it at first, but as the weeks passed, she accepted that it was true. But how hard it was to face the truth: Larry was dead.

Tears welled in her eyes. Her throat dried to parchment as the plane lifted higher and higher. She wanted to call out for comfort, but one look at Sheldon reminded her she mustn't lose her composure. She swallowed her tears and sat up straighter in her seat.

The seat-belt sign shut off, and Beverly felt a mild sense of relief. The plane leveled off. Sheldon was busy writing in his book, and she turned her attention to the view out the window.

The sky was crystal clear. She could see for miles. Below the plane a layer of heavenlike clouds billowed. The expansive view made her gasp.

"Is this your first time in a plane?" Sheldon asked.

"How do you think I got to England from New York?"

Just then the stewardess approached. "Is everything all right?" the pretty girl asked Sheldon.

"Just fine," he answered, his eyebrows raised quizzically as he turned to Beverly. "Are you all right?" She nodded, not trusting her voice.

"Ring if you need anything," the stewardess instructed. "I'll be in the rear cabin. My friends back there have their hands full with three unescorted children and a dozen first-timers." She waved her hand around the empty cabin. "First-class passengers are scarce these days. Will you be all right left alone?"

Sheldon assured her they would be, though Beverly was less confident, especially when the plane lurched suddenly. Beverly cried out in fear.

"It's just the wind. You'll be all right," Sheldon promised her, but the plane lurched again. He caught Beverly in his arms and held her close as the plane fought the rough air pockets. Each time the plane shifted, Sheldon tightened his embrace.

Beverly made a feeble attempt to pull away, but she was as ineffectual at resisting him as she was at calming her racing pulse. Slowly her fear was overshadowed by the fiery sensation building inside her, and she knew fighting him would only add to her anguish. She gave in to the comfort of his arms, hoping he wouldn't take advantage of her vulnerability.

She looked into Sheldon's eyes as the ache inside her mounted. She was uncomfortably aware of how desperately she wanted his lips against hers. His first kiss had released a hunger she had never known before. Of course it hadn't satisfied her desire. She wanted more. Her mounting passion made her tremble uncontrollably.

Sheldon brought her closer to him, sought her mouth with his, and fueled the fire of passion surging deep within her. He kissed her relentlessly, as if he, too, had been starved for her lips. Her hands explored his muscular back, his strong arms, trailed down the front of his shirt, feeling his powerful chest beneath her fingertips; only a thin silk shirt separated her touch and his skin. She caressed his neck, touched his face with her hand. Her thoughts blurred. Her lips parted to receive his kiss more fully. He traced the inside of her lower lip with the tip of his tongue, then his mouth hardened, demanding more, taking more. Their lips merged into one, and Beverly met his passion with a fire of her own, lost beyond protest, a slave to each and every new sensation. She was mindless, without will to his erotic demands, wanting nothing more than for his mouth to continue exploring her fevered body. Her hunger was beyond question, and she was certain he knew it. Even if he didn't love her, she had to have him kiss her like this. She hated herself for the intense burning, but she couldn't deny it no matter how much she wanted to. Thank heaven Larry couldn't see her now.

Suddenly she broke away. Larry! How could she have thought to give herself to Sheldon Whitney? The very idea made her cringe. She had very nearly destroyed her sacred bond with Larry for a casual fling with a man who changed women like shirts, a different one for every day of the week, using them only to satisfy his physical need. She buried her face in her hands and wept.

"What's wrong, Bev?" Sheldon asked quietly, his voice soft, caring. He studied her for a minute while she dried her tears. She ran her hands over her clothes, straightened her blouse and her disheveled hair. "You can't expect me to believe you don't want me," he went on, "when your body is *still* quivering with passion."

"I want you to leave me alone," she said simply but firmly. She had control again. This time she wouldn't lose it.

Sheldon studied her silently. "Perhaps you don't like me,

Miss Milford," he said evenly, his words like daggers in Beverly's heart, for she knew her own words had been lies, first to herself, then to him. "I can't make you care for me. But you must listen to your body. It says otherwise. At least part of you wants me as badly as I want you." His voice had lost the warmth and concern it had held minutes before. "I don't need your love. I don't even seek it," he told her, his voice harsh, unfeeling. "But you have excited my passion—and you must satisfy that, for yourself and for me!"

"I don't feel—" Beverly started to protest.

"I know you, Beverly," he interrupted. "Perhaps better than you know yourself. If you insist on saving your love for just one, then give it to me, not some bloke who'll never quench your fire." Beverly stared at him in silence, unable to speak. "I'll marry you, if that's what it takes," he said angrily. "But don't deny the passion between us. It's been there from the start. Give in, Beverly. Yield to what you know to be true." Beverly couldn't believe her ears. Was Sheldon Whitney proposing marriage? Did he want her body so much that he was willing to give up his freedom to marry her? Hundreds of girls would jump at the chance to have this man all to themselves for a lifetime. Yet Beverly doubted Sheldon would ever be exclusive in his lovemaking, marriage or not. He might be willing to "pay" for what he wanted by marrying, but she would never parody the vows she had made with Larry. She might not be able to control her hunger for Sheldon, but she would never marry without mutual love.

"Is that your price, Bev? Just name the date. We can be married when we land in Paris. It doesn't matter either way to me," he told her.

"How dare you," she hissed. "How could you think of marrying without love?"

"Because I want you," he said plainly. "Very badly." His bold look penetrated her body, igniting her passion despite herself. She knew that she wanted him too. She returned his hungry look, and a satisfied smile spread across his face. He rang for the stewardess. Beverly blushed with humiliation and self-contempt. Obviously he felt nothing. The shame was all hers. Larry would never . . .

She caught herself comparing them again, just moments after she had soiled his memory by an unpardonable comparison. Larry had loved her. Sheldon did not. It was true she had never felt anything like this with her late husband, but sex wasn't everything. Larry had cared for her; Sheldon cared for only one thing.

The stewardess returned in seconds, wheeling a cart with a silver bucket filled with ice, a glistening green bottle protruding from the top. Sheldon lifted the dripping bottle of champagne, examined the label, and handed it to the stewardess to uncork. The loud bang of celebration interrupted the tense silence.

Sheldon expertly caught the foam in a glass before it spilled onto the floor. He handed one glass to Beverly—she had no choice but to accept—and filled another for himself. Almost formally, he touched his glass to hers. The ring of crystal sent shivers down her spine. "To our future," Sheldon toasted before draining his glass.

For however long it may last, Beverly thought to herself. She touched the cool glass to her burning lips and drank the bubbly wine in great gulps, hoping it would help drown her desire.

chapter 3

THE REST OF the trip was a blur of refills of champagne, a bumpy landing, a crowded airport. Beverly gave herself over to Sheldon's care, and he escorted her from the terminal to the limousine that awaited them at the curb. She protested that they had forgotten their luggage, but Sheldon assured her it would reach the hotel before they did.

Inside the car she sat close beside him and rested her drowsy head on his shoulder. When she opened her eyes, they were in front of a magnificent line of hotels and shops, right in the center of Paris.

"Here we are!" Sheldon announced and propelled her through the lobby of their hotel.

She waited to one side while he registered them at the front desk. The two-tiered lobby was peopled with fashionably attired women and their escorts. Brightly colored bouquets filled every corner, and in the center of the room a cast-iron sea nymph spewed water over her bare shoulder, which ran down her arched back and into a pool at her feet. Beverly tingled with excitement to be in Paris.

They rode in the gilded elevator cage to the eighth floor,

silently approving the luxury around them.

"I've never seen anything so grand," Beverly confessed when they reached the top floor of the hotel.

The porter deposited Beverly's luggage in the room, and Sheldon tipped him generously. As soon as they were alone, Beverly found herself suddenly very shy. She waited for Sheldon to renew the passion they had begun in the airplane. Her eyes met his; she closed her eyes and, her face uplifted, waited for him to take her in his arms, to press his mouth against hers. But instead of the fire she had come to expect, Sheldon kissed her with affection. "There will be plenty of time for that later," he said, and Beverly tried to mask her embarrassment, not to mention her disappointment. "I have work to do before dinner," he explained. "The entire trip to Paris will be useless if we fail to sign a contract. We dine with the Couteaus at eight, and I expect you to be especially sharp tonight. Get some sleep now. I'll be back at seven."

This was *not* what Beverly had expected! What had happened to the lust he had shown on the plane? How could he think of business when an hour before his desire had been so powerful he had proposed marriage? Could he have tired of her already, seeing how easily she had been won? Her cheeks burned with humiliation. "Where are you going?" she blurted.

"To my room," he said, surprised. He took her into his arms and held her for a second. "I'm just down the hall if you need me." He smiled, and Beverly felt the fire again. He might have lost interest, but she hadn't. Yet if he was going to be so casual, she would be too.

"Good," she said evenly. "I was afraid you had decided to share my suite."

"Then neither of us would be sharp at dinner tonight," he teased. "Besides, this trip is business first. We have no reason for being here if not to work. You and I can find time for each other after hours. Now sleep," he instructed.

"Dream of me," he added seductively as he closed the door behind him.

"Oh, you are so damn vain," Beverly said out loud, but he didn't hear her. So he was playing it cool. Well, she would, too. He wouldn't get a rise out of her again. That would only assure him she was willing to be an "after-hours" affair, and Beverly valued herself too much to be treated so lightly.

She slipped out of her high-heeled shoes and ran barefoot through the large, plush suite, exploring it as if it were a jungle; magical, lush, exotic. The suite was enormous—and beautiful, as if it had been designed especially to her taste. The ceilings were high, the walls papered in tiny blue and white flowers. A gentle breeze parted the white lace curtains to reveal a large balcony which overlooked a courtyard.

Beverly tore herself away from the garden view below to explore the rest of the suite. There was a sofa in the sitting room, a darker blue than the carpet but lighter than the color on the walls. A single modern painting splashed bold color in the otherwise provincial room.

Behind the door was a bedroom. A high, white canopy bed—feminine but not too frilly—dominated the room. Beyond was a dressing room with a chaise longue and a mirrored wardrobe. In the bathroom a six-foot-long tub sat on four brass bear claws; the floors and walls were marble, and the basins were porcelain with brass fixtures. She started the water in the tub before unpacking her clothes and putting them in the mirrored armoire.

She slipped out of her traveling clothes and into a floor-length bathrobe that felt simply luxurious over her bare skin. Until now Beverly had felt foolish wearing it. She had admired it on one of her infrequent shopping trips with Jancie, and her roommate had gone back to buy it. When she had tried it on she'd been pleased, but secretly she felt silly in the chilly London flat dressed like a Paris model.

Now it was absolutely right, she thought, and she took it off to sink into the deliciously warm, scented bathwater.

All the tension disappeared from her tired body. The room smelled of rosewater, and for a moment Beverly felt confident that everything would work out with Sheldon. She had made a fool of herself on the plane, but that was past. Sheldon would see that she too had come to her senses and was again professional. They would sign the Couteau contract, shake hands on a job well done, and resume the formality that had kept their emotions in check. She finished her bath, toweled herself dry with a thick blue towel, and returned to her bedroom sleepy and happy. She was in Paris. Everything would work out fine!

It seemed she had only just fallen asleep when she heard a knock on the door to her suite. Checking her watch, she found she had slept for over two hours. Could that be Sheldon already? She threw her robe over her warm, sleepy body, tied the knot at the waist, and hurried to answer the door.

"My goodness!" she exclaimed, looking at an armful of daffodils held by a bellhop. "Are these for me?" she asked happily. "From Mr. Whitney?" The young man shook his head, not understanding her English, and held out the flowers for her to take. Beverly tried again. *"Est-ce que ces fleurs sont de Monsieur Whitney?"*

The boy smiled pleasantly at her textbook French and answered her at length, but Beverly couldn't understand what he said, he spoke so fast. She just smiled at him prettily and accepted the flowers. They were the yellowest daffodils she had ever seen.

She found a water pitcher and was arranging the flowers when she heard a second knock at the door. She wondered what the bellhop had forgotten. She swung the door open to find Sheldon standing there, impeccably suited in black evening dress. Beverly caught her breath—he looked so beautiful! How was she ever going to keep her promise to herself to be indifferent?

"Are you going to invite me in?" he asked. "I was hoping you'd be ready, but now I'm glad you're not," he said suggestively. "If the meeting weren't so critical, I'd suggest we skip it altogether. Bev, you look good enough to drive a man to ruin."

She didn't understand this man at all, Beverly thought. One minute he was making love to her, the next he was businesslike, indifferent. Which should she respond to? "I'll be ready in just a minute," she told him hesitantly, clutching at her robe.

"We have to be there in an hour. The Couteaus will appreciate our promptness . . . as I would appreciate yours."

"I'll hurry," Beverly assured him and walked quickly to the bedroom, mindful of his eyes on her slim figure through the thin robe.

Safe behind the bedroom door, she slipped off the silky dressing gown before taking her dress from the closet. As she put on a pair of lace bikini panties she caught sight of herself in the full-length mirror. She knew she would never satisfy the appetite of her sophisticated employer, but she did know her figure was attractive. She ran her hand timidly down her stomach. She heard Sheldon pacing in the other room as she slipped the gown over her head.

Nervously she adjusted the flimsy straps on her bare shoulders before looking at herself in the mirror. Draped in Jancie's elegant cinnamon-red dress, Beverly could do little more than gasp in dismay. How could she possibly enter the living room with Sheldon standing there, much less go to the home of the famous Couteaus in this next-to-nothing costume? How could she ever convince Sheldon Whitney—or herself—that she hadn't planned to wear such a seductive dress?

She forced herself to take another look in the mirror and

pulled the straps a little higher. Still the bodice line was dangerously low. The dress had no back to it, leaving her exposed to the waist.

She hurried across the room, and to her further horror, the dress clung mercilessly when she moved, accentuating each curve of her body. She panicked as she heard Sheldon pacing nervously in the other room. It was too late to consider another dress. She would just have to live with it. She retouched the coil of hair on top of her head. Resignedly she slipped into her shoes, searched the room frantically for her wrap, then remembered that the porter had hung it in the entry hall closet. Knowing she could stall no longer, she grabbed her purse, holding it high in a vain attempt to conceal her exposed bosom, and bravely opened the door to the other room.

Sheldon was lighting a cigarette when Beverly entered the room, but he extinguished it when he saw her. "Time well spent," he finally said, grinning. "You look exquisite. May I help you with your wrap?"

"Please," Beverly said shyly. He draped the black cloth coat onto her shoulders, but even beneath the coat she felt naked to his eye.

"What a shame to cover you up," Sheldon said, continuing to tease. "Monsieur Couteau will be delighted with your dress."

"I thought you said he was married," Beverly said. She took his arm, and they walked toward the elevator.

"Has that ever stopped a man from enjoying what he looks at?" he asked playfully. "Besides," he continued, "his wife welcomes competition from other women. It feeds the fire, she says, and both Celeste and André enjoy a heated affair to a cool liaison."

"How can she be so secure?" Beverly asked incredulously.

"You'll understand when you see her. Few women come

close to challenging her beauty." Sheldon pondered a minute. "Of course, you might give her a real contest dressed the way you are."

Beverly felt her cheeks flush again. "He won't even notice my dress," she said uncertainly. "He designs gowns for the most beautiful models in Europe. He won't even look twice at me or my dress."

"I think you're in for a surprise," Sheldon said.

They walked through the lobby of the hotel. People stopped to look at them, whispering as they passed. Beverly held her head high, trying not to tremble, and took Sheldon's arm for security. His words had made her nervous, and knowing that Couteau would in fact notice her dress made her dread the evening altogether.

Sheldon ushered her into the car and sat dangerously close to her. Beverly folded her hands in her lap and turned a cool shoulder to Sheldon. "You'll do well to please Couteau," he told her.

"I thought we were here on business," Beverly retorted, holding firmly on to her businesslike facade.

"Definitely! But you see, *ma chérie*, the French are known for indulging all their senses, whether at work or play. We'll discuss business tonight, but only for a moment. The rest of the evening will be given to pleasure."

The seriousness with which he spoke made Beverly even more anxious. She tried to answer lightly, but her voice gave her away. "Shall I seduce Mr. Couteau, then?"

"No, my lovely Beverly," Sheldon said earnestly, and Beverly sighed in relief. Sheldon chuckled to himself. "No, you must let André seduce you."

Beverly's smile disappeared. She decided he wasn't kidding. "I hope I won't disappoint you."

"On the contrary, I'm sure you will please me. Especially if you fulfill the promise of that dress," he said huskily. Beverly blushed. "Yes, do that. The color in your cheeks heightens your appeal. You will definitely please Monsieur Couteau."

Beverly's head whirled in confusion. More than anything she wanted to be home, in her own clothes, her emotions calm once again. She tried to quiet the persistent pounding of her heart by looking out the window, but that didn't help. Up and down the boulevard couples strolled, their arms wrapped around each other; beneath a lamp a couple embraced, oblivious to the world. "Are we nearly there?" she asked Sheldon to fill the embarrassed silence.

"Yes," he said. He had seen the couples too, had seen Beverly watching them. "I was beginning to wonder if I would have to call off the dinner and feast on you alone. Another five minutes alone in this car and I would have thrown caution to the wind."

"Business first," Beverly reminded him, sounding more confident and assured than she felt.

"Business first," he agreed. He looked at her directly. "But for dessert . . ."

Beverly lowered her eyes to the floor of the car. She could feel his eyes on her, waiting for an answer. The decision was hers. If she didn't answer, and quickly, he might misinterpret her silence as an agreement to his plans. "Surely you can wait that long—at least until you have the contract signed," she said, attempting a flirtatious air. Sheldon eyed her suspiciously.

"Miss Milford, I hope you know yourself better than to promise something you aren't prepared to deliver."

Beverly fought to maintain the bantering tone. "I make no promises, Mr. Whitney. I learned that from you."

"Sometimes I wonder if you learned too much from me," he said.

"Perhaps you should tell me about the Couteaus," Beverly said to change the subject. "I'll want to know how to approach them."

Sheldon looked at her appraisingly. "I'm not sure what to tell you. I don't know if I'm talking to cool Beverly from the office or this fiery lady you've become since leaving London. Really, Beverly, you should get away more often."

"Perhaps you should simply describe the Couteaus and keep your eyes open during the evening for clues to the answers to your questions." She was stunned by the flippancy of her own words, the casual, provocative tone of her voice. But if she gave in now she'd never make it through the evening. As it was, Sheldon knew of her passion for him. The only hope she had was to call his bluff, to treat the matter as casually as he. He might lose interest in the game quickly, before it cost Beverly any more than it already had.

"Be careful, Beverly," he warned.

"Of you? Or the Couteaus?" she asked ingenuously.

"Of yourself," he said deliberately, just as the car reached 20 Tesman Avenue. The driver opened the door for Beverly; Sheldon's leg grazed hers as he followed her out of the car, sending renewed sensations up and down her body.

They stood in front of a formidable row of old stone houses, each four stories high, each elaborately decorated with wrought-iron. As beautiful as the ornate banisters were, Beverly sensed that their purpose was to isolate, to keep people out rather than welcome guests in. The front of each building was cold and impersonal, Beverly noticed, and wondered how, in the richest section of Paris, the architecture could be so hostile.

"This way," Sheldon said, taking her elbow and guiding her around the house to an enormous gate. A gatekeeper unlocked the huge portal to let them pass. A cobblestoned pathway opened onto a magnificent courtyard with lawn so green that Beverly was sure no one had ever stepped on it. Dark green shrubs surrounded the lawn; flowers grew in rows at the base of the shrubs. There were two shade trees, and in the middle of the lawn was a motionless statue of a fish with silver gills.

The sky was turning dark save for a sliver of moon.

"Oh, Sheldon, isn't this beautiful?" Beverly asked.

He looked at the moon and touched Beverly's shining hair. "Yes, it is. You look lovely tonight," he said tenderly.

Beverly was touched by the sincerity of his voice. He constantly surprised her. Did he scorn her, as she suspected? Or care for her, as he suggested now?

She studied his handsome face, so near to her own. She wanted to reach out and touch him, but she knew she didn't dare. In another minute they would be meeting the Couteaus. The entire success of the trip rested on this evening. Sheldon would never forgive her if she lost her head tonight. Her only chance, she knew now, was to convince Sheldon that her feelings were as casual as his own. She would flirt with André. She would keep the tone light and enjoyable and do her best to help him secure the contract.

She looked again at Sheldon's face before replacing her mask of indifference. It was a tighter fit this time, now that she understood her feelings. As she stood under the soft moonlight in this magical garden, her heart spoke to her loudly. It might be true that Sheldon didn't care for her, but she yearned for him. It was his love she wanted. She wanted him to quiet her loneliness as well as her passion. The passion was but an expression of the love she felt for him. She couldn't separate the two. She also knew, realistically, that she could expect only the first from him. She must never expect his love or his constant attention. Even his marriage proposal had been flippant, void of love but full of lust. If she could have fought her love, she would have. But that was impossible. Numbly she followed Sheldon through the patio to the Couteaus' front door.

chapter 4

HE RANG the bell twice. In a moment the door swung open, and a petite, zephyrlike woman of incomparable beauty expressed her delight at seeing him. She covered him with enthusiastic kisses, all the while declaring her joy in rapid-fire French. Sheldon returned her warm greeting, embracing the French beauty with all his strength. Beverly felt invisible—and wished she were.

The tiny woman peered from beneath thick, black bangs and surveyed Beverly suspiciously, judging her with cat-green eyes. She turned to Sheldon and whispered something naughty into his ear, then pouted when he responded with hearty laughter. Her expression changed again, just as abruptly, as she snuggled back into his arms and let herself be cuddled.

Sheldon smiled wickedly as he caught the undisguised look of jealousy on Beverly's face.

"You're right, Celeste," he said in perfect French, smoothing a tangle of curls with one hand. "She is very beautiful. Let us take her inside for André to enjoy. I'll introduce you all at once."

In the living room Celeste stood between pillars of stately good looks—Sheldon and a boyishly handsome Frenchman, undoubtedly André. He rushed forward, took both of Beverly's hands in his, and bowed deeply, brushing his lips delicately against her hand, making her shiver. He straightened to her exact height and looked her directly in the eye. "I am André," he said simply. "And you are a rare beauty. Sheldon," he said, not taking his eyes from Beverly, "you spoke truthfully."

Beverly had to laugh at his directness. His boyish charm was not diminished by his formal evening attire: a white shirt, lacy and frilled, and a rich black velvet jacket which fit snuggly, emphasizing his youthful figure. His silky black hair fell across his doe-brown eyes. He looked to be seventeen years old, but Beverly knew, judging from the number of international awards he had received for his dress design, that he must be twice that age.

She turned to Celeste. "Your home is beautiful."

Celeste bubbled with delight and spun around, her arms outstretched in excitement, her black silk dress flaring as she turned. "It is all Andfe's work," she confessed proudly. "I am useless at decorating. He is the artist. I am but a silly housewife."

André quickly contradicted. "I can do nothing without her," he insisted. They exchanged a look of love that made Beverly ache. "But I am a miserable host," he apologized. "I have let my guests stand without beverage. What will you like to drink?" he asked Beverly.

"White wine?" she replied, hoping she had asked for something simple.

He pulled a heavy-braided cord to summon the servant. "Celeste?" he said. "What will you have to drink?"

"I will drink the same as our pretty guest, *mon chéri*," she said.

"Fine. And you," he said, turning to Sheldon, "what would you like, my long-absent friend?"

"Whiskey," Sheldon said matter-of-factly. He leaned against the dark wooden mantel.

When the wine was brought André expertly uncorked the bottle. He tasted a drop, then poured the sparkling white liquid into fragile long-stemmed wineglasses. "Mademoiselle," he said to Beverly, handing her a full glass. "Madame," he said, repeating the gesture for his wife, adding a kiss. He poured two generous portions of whiskey for Sheldon and himself, then all four raised their glasses to each other and drank.

Celeste took Beverly by the hand and led her to a green velvet sofa.

"You're so lucky," Beverly said, sincerely moved by André's display of affection. "He is so thoughtful," she added wistfully, hesitantly shifting her glance to the fireplace where Sheldon and André stood talking. Sheldon returned her stare, his long gaze lingering over her body. She turned away, hoping Celeste hadn't noticed, only to find her smiling openly.

"And you," Celeste whispered gleefully, "you, too, are fortunate."

Beverly was puzzled, but Celeste went on to explain.

"To have Sheldon Whitney in love with you," she said, rolling her eyes upward and gesturing with her left hand. Beverly started to explain that Sheldon was far from in love with her, or with any one woman, but Celeste had no mind to listen. "After so many girls have tried to capture his heart," she added.

"No," Beverly said. As much as she wanted to believe Celeste's words, she had to set her straight. "I only work for him."

"But you are wrong, of course," Celeste assured her.

"He cannot take his eyes from you."

Beverly had to laugh. "That's not *love*," she said. "It's this dress!"

"No," Celeste insisted. "At first I thought you were but a new plaything, but I have seen now how he looks at you, and it is love. Have you seen how André looks at me?"

"How could I help but notice?" Beverly asked, recalling the unmistakable love in his eyes.

"But that is how Sheldon looks at you! It is true, even if you can't see it. Believe me," she implored, ignoring Beverly's silent denial, "I know Sheldon well. He looks at you with love."

"What are you two beauties so serious about?" André asked, walking over to them. Standing behind the sofa, he rested both hands on Celeste's shoulders.

"We are neglected," she answered, pouting. "You do not love us."

André tilted his head to one side. His eyes twinkled knowingly. "But of course you are loved," he assured her, echoing Celeste's words to Beverly. "How can you doubt that?" Sheldon had followed André to the sofa and now stood beside him, watching the domestic exchange.

Celeste turned her attention to Sheldon. "No," she said sadly, repeating her charge to Sheldon. "André neglects me. And you neglect your Beverly." She bit her lip playfully.

"How do we neglect you?" Sheldon asked, walking around the sofa and taking a seat beside Celeste.

"Why, we have finished our wine so long ago, and no one has thought to refill our empty glasses."

"Simple to remedy," Sheldon said, getting up and bringing the bottle of wine from the table. He filled Celeste's glass, then Beverly's. "There, is that better?" he asked. "Do you feel loved now?"

Celeste winked at Beverly. "Much better, thank you."

"And you, Beverly?" Sheldon asked, turning to face her

directly. "You don't feel neglected now, do you?"

"Of course she does," Celeste answered before Beverly could speak for herself, even if she had known what to answer. "If I were not so happily married to André, I would implore him to look after her himself. But I need him so very badly that *you* must look after her!"

"Do you feel neglected?" Sheldon asked Beverly again.

"How can I possibly feel neglected," she managed to ask, her voice light with a buoyancy she didn't feel, "with all this attention? Two handsome men concerned with my well-being, and the friendship and care of beautiful Celeste. What more could I ask for?" She lifted her wineglass in a toast to their kindness. They clinked glasses again, and Beverly drank the wine eagerly, the cool, clear Chablis sliding like water down her parched throat.

"Careful," Sheldon said quietly, noticing the flush on her smooth pale skin. "I'll take care of you, but I'd rather not carry you home."

Defiantly, Beverly tossed back the remaining wine in her glass. His concern stirred her deeply, but she dared not show it. "You won't have to," she promised. She watched his mouth tighten in disapproval.

She felt light-headed as she stood up and walked around the sofa to stand beside André. In timid French she asked him if he would pour her another glass of wine. He took the bottle from Sheldon and graciously filled Beverly's glass again. Celeste left to confer with the cook about dinner. Beverly knew Sheldon was watching her, but she chose to ignore him, turning her attention to André. "Do you ever travel to England?" she asked, both out of curiosity and for something to say.

"Once or twice a year," he told her. "I like the Christmas festivities of the English. And British theater is superior. Do you like the theater?" he asked.

"Oh, very much," Beverly bubbled. "I don't have much

opportunity to go, however—we're so busy. I used to see plays on Broadway," she added, not wanting to sound self-pitying.

"Ahhh," André exclaimed. "The wonderful musicals. Whenever I think of America, I think of the people with their voices raised in song." Beverly had to laugh, for she remembered New York in a different light. "We will go to the theatre together when I next come to London."

"Oh, yes, let's," Beverly said enthusiastically. "When do you think you can come?"

"Are you inviting him as your guest?" Sheldon asked, rather tartly, Beverly thought. She looked at him critically, and he gave her a look as disapproving as hers.

"Celeste and I would love to visit you," André continued joyfully, ignoring Sheldon's tone. "But then you are not British. You are American, yes?"

Beverly nodded and sipped her wine.

"Entirely," Sheldon interjected, his voice cutting, unfriendly. Beverly wondered at his harshness, and when she turned she saw him lift his glass and finish the amber liquid in one swallow.

"British women are not so naive, or so unpredictable," Sheldon said, getting up to pour himself another whiskey.

"Only British *men* are unpredictable," André retorted, coming to Beverly's defense, his voice light with laughter. At that moment Celeste returned to announce dinner.

André offered Beverly his arm before Sheldon had a chance, and together they followed Celeste past the double carved doors and into the formal dining room. A dozen candles flickered down the center of the table, but when Beverly's eyes adjusted to the candlelight she saw that their four places had been set at one end, creating intimacy.

André seated Beverly to his right, the place of honor, and directed Sheldon to sit across from her, on Celeste's left.

The food was superb, excellently prepared and beautifully served. André filled Beverly's glass with wine before the first course and continued to fill it with each course, despite her protests. The conversation was easy and light. Sometimes the four of them talked to each other, but more often André monopolized Beverly and Celeste entertained Sheldon.

André continued to question Beverly about herself as they carried their coffee and brandy into the salon. She talked about the differences between New York and London, the challenge of adjusting. "What about Paris?" he asked her.

"We only just arrived," she explained. "I haven't seen anything of the city yet."

"Sheldon," André said, "what kind of tour have you planned for Mademoiselle Milford? She claims she hasn't seen anything of our city."

"That's right. We went straight to the hotel from the airport."

"And tomorrow?" André pressed. Beneath his boyish charm Beverly saw the strength that had made him an international powerhouse in fashion design.

"I'm afraid there's too much business on this trip," Sheldon explained, careful to keep the apology from his voice. "Perhaps at the weekend, if there's time. Or on the next trip."

"Nonsense," André pronounced. "You cannot bring a beautiful women to Paris in springtime and make her work all day. There must be time to show her the sights."

"Remember," Celeste interjected, "this is her first trip to our beautiful city. Just because you are traveled, Sheldon, you cannot forget the first time you came to Paris, and the tour you had."

"I'm afraid we're very busy now," Sheldon repeated.

"I had expected to work," Beverly volunteered, coming

to Sheldon's aid. "That's the reason I was brought along."

André acted as if he hadn't heard Beverly. "If you insist she work, Sheldon, then I insist that a tour of our shops is essential if you want to represent our fall line of fashion." He looked at Sheldon as he spoke, his voice challenging him to differ. "We will talk business only after I have had a chance to win Beverly over to my side. Who else will see that my interests are met in the contract? Surely not you, Sheldon. We know each other too well to assume that." His eyes sparkled shrewdly. He turned to Celeste, his manner softened. "Darling, will you conduct the tour?"

"But of course," Celeste agreed, delighted with her husband's plan. "And Sheldon, you will join us first for lunch?"

"I'm afraid I must work tomorrow, no matter how much André protests. But do enjoy yourselves!" His lips curled in a smile, and Beverly thought he might not be upset with the plan after all. Perhaps she could use the time to persuade André and Celeste to accept Sheldon's terms for the contract.

"*Sacré bleu!*" Celeste exclaimed excitedly, throwing her hand to her forehead. "I have forgotten! I must meet Monsieur Frederik tomorrow at noon. And he is two hours south by train," she explained to Beverly. "I will not be back until late in the day."

Sheldon shrugged. "Guess you'll be working after all," he said to Beverly with malicious satisfaction.

"No, no," André protested. "I will conduct the tour myself." This time it was André who smiled smugly.

"You?" Sheldon laughed incredulously. "With your busy schedule?"

"I am never too busy to entertain a beautiful lady on her first trip to Paris," he said proudly. "It is too bad you are so busy yourself." He stared at Sheldon, a gleam of superiority in his eye, then turned to Beverly. "Do you mind so terribly, Beverly?"

"Of course not!" she assured him. She was flattered that he would want to take time with her, but she wished Sheldon didn't look so glum. "There's nothing I would rather have tomorrow than the Couteau personal tour."

"Fine," Sheldon announced, standing up and checking his wristwatch. "But if you want to be rested tomorrow, we must return to the hotel now."

Beverly was disappointed. The evening was still young and she was having such a good time, but if Sheldon thought they should leave, he knew best.

"I wish you were coming with us," Beverly told Celeste, as they stood in the hallway retrieving her wrap.

"I only care that you love Paris as I do, so you will return soon and often," Celeste assured her. "Good night, my friend," she said to Beverly, kissing both sides of her face. She turned to Sheldon and kissed him, a devilish smile on her lips. "And good night to you, my friend."

"Good night, and thank you for everything," Beverly and Sheldon said at once.

Outside the town house Beverly adjusted her coat around her shoulders. She was glad for the fresh air; the wine had made her head spin, and the overheated apartment hadn't helped. She inhaled deeply as they walked back to the street.

When they reached the curb, André's driver was holding the door to the sleek black limousine open for them. Beverly snuggled into the rich, fragrant leather, glad for the dark. She leaned back and closed her eyes, remembering the conversation of the evening. Perhaps Celeste was right. Perhaps Sheldon did care for her a little and was waiting for a sign from her. How could she tell him without compromising herself, or her resolve to keep distant from his physical charms? She opened her eyes to look at him, but his profile was impossible to read. She closed her eyes again, wondering if she dared to dream of his love.

When the car stopped in front of the hotel, Beverly was

jarred out of her reverie. She accepted Sheldon's hand and stepped out onto the pavement. Her heel caught in a crack, and she tripped, grabbing Sheldon's arm to upright herself.

She started to thank him when she caught the look of disgust in his eye. "I didn't bring you to Paris to make a spectacle of yourself," he told her brutally. "Have you had too much to drink?"

"How dare you ask such a thing? I've never been drunk in my life!" She reached down for her broken heel and thrust it in his face. He stared at her in disbelief. "You are not a gentleman!" she said indignantly and hobbled away. He followed her without saying anything.

She cursed him silently while they waited for the elevator. How could she have ever thought he cared for her? The reverse was so clearly true. The elevator came at last, and Beverly stepped in, ignoring Sheldon. She stared at the floor and stepped out quickly when they reached the top floor.

They reached Sheldon's room first, but neither of them paused to stop. Beverly fumbled for her room key in her evening bag and fit it into the lock. She turned to bid Sheldon a hasty good night, but he pushed the door open and entered, leaving Beverly to follow.

"I'm really very tired," she said coldly, reaching down to rub her swollen ankle. The room was stuffy, and Beverly unbuttoned her coat and hung it in the closet, then crossed the room to open the doors to the terrace.

"Skip the excuses, Bev," he said abruptly, grabbing her arm as she passed.

"Sheldon, you're hurting me," she pleaded, but he ignored her cry and silenced her protests by covering her mouth with his. All evening she had dreamed of his kiss, but not like this! Not when he so clearly scorned her, had accused her of drunkenness. She would not let him touch her, despite the passion she had felt for him earlier.

She fought to break away from him, but she was helpless against his brute force. "Stop it," she cried, but he silenced her again with his hard, demanding mouth. His tense body pressed against hers, and she felt her heart racing despite her reluctance, her resistance and anger melting, the passion of the afternoon returning.

"Give in, Beverly," he coaxed. "You want me as much as I want you."

He held her tightly, pinning her arms to her side with his powerful arms. His kiss was abrupt and hard, wringing from her a deep, distressed sob.

He let her go after what seemed an eternity. Beverly felt her body go limp. Then the trembling turned to anger. She stared at him furiously. "How dare you!" she fumed.

A slow, challenging smile formed on his face. "You don't look like you minded too much, Bev. You look like you want me to stay the night with you. Would you have let André stay the night, if you could have persuaded Celeste to look the other way? Don't you let your British boyfriend keep you warm through the cold London nights?"

Beverly staggered to the sofa and collapsed on it. What on earth was he talking about? Had he gone mad? She had not so much as looked at the men in the office, except to be courteous. Did he think she would feign friendship with Celeste while intending to steal her husband? How could Celeste have ever thought Sheldon loved her? Clearly he hated and scorned her. "You suspect André, and others, because wantonness runs rampant in your own life," she told him bitterly when she had gathered her wits enough to speak. "Not everybody seeks variety the way you do," she added contemptuously.

Sheldon stared at her, his eyes blazing with anger, too angry to respond. He grabbed the vase full of flowers and let it fall to the floor, then, without a word, walked out the door, slamming it behind him.

Beverly stared at the broken vase and strewn flowers. She didn't know what had happened. Nothing made sense. She gathered the daffodils into her arms sadly and found another container for them, but they had lost their beauty to Sheldon's cruelty. She left them in the sitting room and turned on the light in the bedroom. Someone had turned down her bed, and left two chocolate mints on her pillowcase. How like the French, she thought, removing her evening gown and hanging it in the armoire. But the discovery did little to lighten her mood.

She rummaged impatiently through the top dresser drawer until she found her sheer pink lace nightgown. She slipped it on and turned out the lights, determined to sleep at once, to erase the unpleasantness of Sheldon's behavior from her mind.

She lay in the dark, her eyes clenched as tightly as her fists at her side, but all she could think about was Sheldon's peculiar behavior. His words and his actions kept running through her head, again and again, without getting any clearer.

Suddenly she knew she had to talk to him. She sprang out of bed and dressed quickly. This time she felt comfortable wearing the spicy-red dress that had made her feel so uneasy earlier in the evening. She grabbed her purse and checked for her key. Touching her hand to her hair, she found it still in place. She locked the door behind her and hurried toward Sheldon's room.

The hallway was empty. She checked her watch to find that it was after one o'clock. She tapped lightly on his door, and when no one answered she knocked again, this time louder. Again her reply was silence. Beverly wondered if he had already gone to sleep. It would be just like him to set her mind on edge but to find sleep peacefully himself.

She was about to return to her room but changed her mind, deciding to go downstairs to the cocktail lounge instead. A brandy would soothe her to sleep. It was just what she needed, she thought as she rang for the elevator.

The cocktail lounge was dark when she arrived, and it was several moments before her eyes adjusted. In the distance she recognized Sheldon's voice, filled with animation. Perfect, Beverly thought. She could talk to him here. It would be better than his rooms, anyway, less intimate.

She stumbled through the dark room and found him perched on a bar stool. Before she reached him, however, she saw he wasn't alone. An exotic-looking woman was at his side. Both were laughing at something Sheldon had said.

Beverly felt her heart stop as she watched them. She spun around blindly to flee the room, hoping Sheldon hadn't seen her.

At the door, she heard him call out after her. Let him call, she thought angrily. She wouldn't answer. From now on, whatever happened between them would be strictly business. She had been a fool to think of him in any other way. She had been right to keep her heart locked away. The gentle love she had known with Larry was the last she would ever feel.

chapter 5

THE DAYLIGHT SHONE through the frail white curtains, spreading a filtered glow across the room. She stretched lazily like a cat in the sunlight, enjoying the warmth of her bed. She must have slept soundly, for she didn't remember waking except once, somewhere in the middle of the night. She had heard a faint knocking at her door, a voice calling in the distance, but when she sat up to listen the night had returned to silence. Guessing she had been dreaming, she fell back to sleep. Now, in the bright light of morning, she was certain it was a dream.

She stretched one more time, arching her long, slender back against the silky sheets. Then, excited at the prospect of her tour of Paris and her chance to convince André to let Whitney-Forbes represent Couteau's line of fashion, she threw off the lavender quilted comforter and sprang out of bed.

While the bathwater ran she selected a pale blue wool dress and a burgundy scarf to wear. For a moment Beverly wondered if she would look out of place at André's salon. She paused in front of the mirror and pressed the dress against her body, pleased with what she saw. She might never be worldly, the way Sheldon preferred his women, but she had decided not to worry about his likes and dislikes. André would appreciate her style. His designs were world-famous for their simplicity.

Before she slipped into the bath, she ordered a continental breakfast sent up to her room. She wanted to avoid Sheldon until after she had had a chance to talk with André about the contract.

She washed and dressed quickly, then sat down for the light meal of café au lait and croissants. The flaky rolls melted in her mouth, and she had to admit that French cooking was far superior to British, in which everything was overcooked and mushy. She dusted the crumbs from her lips with the linen napkin, folded it carefully before returning it to the sterling ring, and left the heavy silver tray by the door. From her bedroom the phone rang. Beverly reached it before the second ring.

"Hello, Beverly?" It was André, and he sounded upset.

"Is there trouble?" she asked at once.

"I am afraid so," he told her apologetically. "My cutter has quit in a rage, and the fitter refuses to work with anyone else. I am afraid I will have to cancel our tour today. Can you forgive me?"

"Of course," Beverly told him, trying to conceal her sharp disappointment. Now she would miss the tour, and her opportunity to secure the contract.

"What will you do today?" he asked. "Can you insist that Monsieur Whitney treat you to a tour after all?"

"I can try," she said brightly, but she knew she would never ask Sheldon for anything, unless it was business. "Or I can do the tour alone."

"I am so very sorry," he told her sadly.

"You mustn't worry," she assured him. In the background she could hear the commotion. She knew that even now she was keeping him from work. "I'll be fine." she insisted, but as she hung up the phone she wondered where to start on her self-guided tour. Nevertheless, she hadn't flown across the English Channel to sit in her hotel room all day.

She left the hotel hastily, uncertain which way to go. The sunlight that had greeted her that morning had been merely a tease. The air was sharply cold along the rue de Rivoli, and the sun did little to help. Still, Beverly thought, it is Paris, and it is beautiful. She hailed a taxi and asked the driver to take her to the Louvre.

The driver, a small, dark mustached man in his forties, smiled at her accent. He spoke to her rapidly over his shoulder, pointing out attractions as they rode through the streets. Beverly was convinced that Paris, with its tulip-lined streets and awesome gray architecture, its street vendors peddling nuts and sandwiches, was the most romantic city she had ever seen.

The driver deposited her at the steps of the marble-columned Louvre, and Beverly quickly counted out the twelve-franc fare, adding three additional francs for a tip, before hurrying inside.

Beverly was amazed at the size of the museum. She didn't know much about art, but the masterpieces awed her. She stood in front of the "Mona Lisa" for a long time, waiting for the famous half-smile to broaden. She looked as if at any moment she would speak and explain the mystery of her secret smile.

Just as she was ready to leave the museum, a crowd of French schoolchildren filled the lobby. Beverly watched them fall into two parallel lines. Her heart swelled at the sight of such well-behaved children, a collection as inspired as the art she had just seen. The boys wore short navy pants; the girls navy skirts. Both wore white tailored shirts.

One tiny girl lost track of her group when she bent to

pull up her white knee sock. When the child noticed that she was alone, she burst into tears. Beverly instinctively moved to comfort the child. She gave her a tight little hug, took hold of her hand, and led her into the room she had seen the class enter. The child shrieked with relief to find her class; the teacher scolded her gently and looked at Beverly thankfully.

Beverly reached the sidewalk feeling very happy. She walked along the Quai du Louvre, enjoying the river, until she reached the Café du Pont-Neuf. As she ordered soup and bread and an entree of moules, she found herself imagining the exquisite child she and Sheldon could produce. She had to laugh at herself in reproach. A child would never suit his frivolous life-style. She reminded herself again of her resolution of the night before, then turned her thoughts to the meal the waiter was placing before her. She hadn't realized how hungry she was, and she ate the delicious food greedily.

By the end of the day Beverly had visited Notre-Dame and the Palais de Justice. She made a final stop at Sainte-Chapelle on her way back. Her feet hurt from so much walking, and she thought she would rest a minute in the tall, old church.

She found it empty except for an old woman dressed in black kneeling at the front of the church. Beverly stood at the back until she left, not wishing to disturb her.

She had never considered herself religious, but she couldn't help feeling inspired in the ancient cathedral. She wondered at what had inspired generations of artists to create buildings of this kind, or the paintings in the Louvre.

It was difficult to find words to express her precise feelings, but she knew it had something to do with the shafts of light that magically supported the high ceilings, the hundreds of stained-glass scenes that united her with a grander time. More importantly, it had something to do with her feelings for Sheldon. As she rose from the pew and felt the light showering in on her through the high colored-glass windows, she knew, for the second time since arriving in Paris, that she loved him. She had tried to deny these feelings, but they were there whether she admitted them or not. When she left the cathedral, she felt calm. It didn't matter that he didn't know. She loved him, totally and completely, as she had never loved before. The sun was setting in the sky as she strolled down the boulevard through the bustling crowds on the rue de Rivoli back to the hotel, back to her love.

That evening she dressed with extra care as she prepared to meet Sheldon for dinner. He had left her a note at the desk asking that she be ready for dinner at eight. That gave her slightly more than an hour, and she used the time to take a long, leisurely bath, dreaming of her journey through the magical city.

She chose a pretty floor-length lemon-colored dress with a lace bodice and spent the remaining minutes with her hair, curling it softly around her face. She finished off her outfit with a single strand of pearls and matching earrings. She had just stepped into her high-heeled shoes, which made her nearly as tall as Sheldon, when he knocked on her door. She checked her lipstick a second time, trying to quiet her heartbeat, before answering his knock.

He was dressed elegantly in a white tuxedo. "Are you ready?" he asked formally. It was the first time they had talked since their quarrel, since she had seen him with that woman in the bar. Beverly could see that his coolness was intentional, and she tried not to let it bother her. She wanted nothing to spoil her wonderful day, her special feelings for him. She accepted his arm as casually as he offered it. Together they left the hotel for La Chandelle.

The maître d' remembered Sheldon from previous visits and gave them a splendid table overlooking the river, away from the crowd. They spoke little during the meal, and Beverly was satisfied with the silence; it gave her peace to enjoy the delicious food, to think about the lovely day. For dessert she ordered crème caramel over a vast assortment of sweets from a tray. Sheldon sipped an espresso, and Beverly enjoyed a cappuccino.

"You must have charmed André today," Sheldon said when they had finished their desserts. Beverly looked at him questioningly. "He called me this afternoon," he explained. "And agreed to sign the contract." Beverly's face lit up at the unexpected news. "Without any objections," Sheldon continued.

"No objections!" Beverly exclaimed in amazement. They had expected to sign Couteau as a client, but only after fighting tooth and nail over specific terms. "What good fortune!" she said happily.

"No objections," Sheldon repeated carefully. He took a quick sip of his brandy, then signaled the waiter to bring the check. "What did you do to him?" he asked suddenly, his voice suspicious.

"Why I—" She started to explain that André had canceled the plans, but Sheldon interrupted her.

"He said he owed you an apology." He watched her, looking for a reaction to his news. "He said he did have one condition to signing the contract—that you must come to his office first thing in the morning. Alone."

"Is that all he said?" Beverly asked, puzzled.

Sheldon nodded. "That's all. I was hoping you would be able to explain," he said with a sneer.

Beverly didn't know what to think. She would understand better after she met with André in the morning. She had better not make any guesses this evening. "I can't imagine what he wants," she said.

"I see," Sheldon said evenly. "I hadn't expected to win this contract so easily," he told her, his voice edged with cynicism. "I had underestimated your power. You are a very *capable* assistant. We'll have to give you a raise, won't we?" Beverly shrugged her slender shoulders. "Now that you have cinched the contract, there is no further reason for our staying in France," he went on coolly. "Especially now that you've had your tour. Did you have a good time, Miss Milford? Is Paris all you thought it would be?"

Beverly wanted to tell him about the wonderful day she had had, about the child in the museum, about the "Mona Lisa," who almost smiled at her; most of all she wanted to tell him about the cathedral. But something in his voice told her he wouldn't be pleased, and she couldn't stand for anything, especially Sheldon's mockery, to tarnish her perfect day. She finished her coffee in silence, her eyes lowered.

They decided to walk back to the hotel, along the avenue. At the door to her room, Sheldon bade her good night. "I expect you'll want a good night's sleep, to be sharp for André at nine o'clock."

Before Beverly could think of a quick reply, he was gone. She let herself into her room and closed the door behind her. When she checked her watch for the time, she found it was only eleven thirty. Her last night in Paris, and she was going to bed before midnight, she thought unhappily. Sheldon, no doubt, had a full evening planned; why else would he have left her so early, standing in the hall, without even trying to kiss her good night? Beverly guessed he was on his way to meet the woman he had picked up the night before.

She removed her clothing slowly, then resignedly climbed into bed. The lights of the city shone through the French windows, reminding her of the lovely city just beyond her reach. It wouldn't do for her to explore the city alone at night, and Sheldon was engaged in another woman's arms. Was this her fate, to love a reckless libertine, to lie alone, night after night, her heart with a mind of its own, beyond her control?

She forced her thoughts to André and Celeste, and what she must say to them the following day. She thought again of the beautiful cathedral, and her silly thoughts about the child she and Sheldon might have had together. Misery replaced the happiness she had felt earlier in the day, and she couldn't stop the stream of tears that dampened her pillow. She cried herself to sleep, knowing that Sheldon possessed her heart. Not only did he not know, but he would never care to know.

chapter 6

THE NEXT MORNING, Beverly dressed quickly and returned her clothes to her suitcase, leaving it at the desk with a note for Sheldon. Their plane left from De Gaulle Airport at one o'clock, and she would have to rush from André's place of business to make the flight on time. She guessed Sheldon would leave from the hotel, and in her note she apologized for giving him the responsibility of her luggage, but she hoped he would understand. She grabbed a taxi, and before she knew it the driver had delivered her to Couteau's shop.

From the outside the building looked just like any other, but inside Beverly was overcome by the enormous sense of wealth, of class, noticeable in both the refined woman who greeted her and took her to André and the glamorous models Beverly saw later in the showrooms. The customers were the most interesting of all to watch, Beverly thought, and made a number of mental notes so that Whitney-Forbes could most accurately represent them. She watched the rich silver-haired gentlemen pamper their youthful girl friends by buying them anything and everything they commented on. Beverly noticed, too, that though some of the older women were not very attractive, dressed in André's gowns they looked actually beautiful. It was the gift of wealth to be able to afford beauty.

André was busy when Beverly arrived, and Celeste was not there yet, so a saleswoman, Colette, showed her around the sizable shop, answering in perfect English all of Beverly's questions. By the end of the tour she understood just what Couteau needed to promote its sales. Sheldon would be proud of her, she thought, then brought her thoughts quickly back to the store.

At last André was free. Celeste had arrived, and together they sat on the rear terrace overlooking the boulevard, sipping morning coffee and biscuits, caviar and tiny pastries.

"I should leave soon," Beverly told them regretfully. "I have to be on the plane at one o'clock, and the airport, as I remember, is a long taxi ride from here." She hated for the visit to end, for she had grown even fonder of the Couteaus.

"Let us drive you to the airport," Celeste suggested. Beverly started to protest. She saw how difficult it was for them to leave their work even for this short break.

Celeste turned to André. "Let us, please. I won't see my Beverly for so long a time, and the taxi is such a rude way to depart the city." Beverly could tell that André was thinking of the hours of work that awaited him, but he gave serious consideration to Celeste's proposition. "Please?" Celeste pressed.

André smiled at Beverly, as if to let her in on a secret, but the influence Celeste had on him was hardly that. "She is right," he said kindly. "You must not leave Paris with your last memory that of our taxi drivers. Of course we will accompany you to the plane."

"Are you sure?" Beverly asked, moved by their generosity.

"Absolutely. Besides, I should like to say adieu to Sheldon. He sounded so distant on the phone yesterday. I had expected to hear him jump for joy, as you people say, at the news of an uncontested contract." He winked at Beverly. "I gave the credit to you, did you know?" Beverly was about to thank him, but André went on. "Perhaps that was what made him distant," he mused. "He is a man who likes to do things alone. He doesn't like to need anyone's help. He will learn, as I have." He took Celeste's small diamonded hand into his and squeezed it lightly. "Without my Celeste there would be no joy, in work or in play." Celeste beamed under his praise, and Beverly couldn't help but feel envy burn deep inside her at this display of love. André directed the two women to the front lobby and promised to meet them there in a moment. The two linked arms and proceeded to the front hallway, pausing on the way to admire the beautiful gowns the models displayed.

The driver was loading two heavy boxes into the trunk of the car as the threesome situated themselves in the back seat of the limousine. Too soon they were in the middle of the airport traffic.

Beverly found Sheldon in a temper. He had just checked his watch and was beginning to wonder if she would make the plane in time. He was prepared to reprimand her but changed his mind when he saw Celeste at her side and André following, a heavy box in his arms. The chauffeur followed him with a second one of equal size. They were a happy group, and their gaiety seemed to irritate Sheldon.

"What is in these boxes?" Sheldon asked. Celeste giggled with delight, and André pretended he didn't know. Sheldon turned to her. "Beverly?" he asked.

Beverly shook her head and smiled. "They won't tell me. It's some kind of secret," she told him truthfully. She had asked the same question on the way to the airport, and it had been met with the same gleeful evasion. Even when the driver unloaded the boxes, Celeste wouldn't tell her the contents. "Please tell us," she urged André. "I can't stand the mystery a minute longer."

"All right," Celeste said joyfully. "But you must look

for yourself!" She reached down and started to untie the string to the box.

"Celeste," André interrupted. "You must let Beverly open them herself."

"Why me?" Beverly asked.

"Because they are all for you," André explained.

"Do you think the airport is the place to open a present?" Sheldon asked skeptically. Their plane was due to depart in a few minutes, and if they missed it, they would have to wait several hours for the next one.

"If you are to know what it is, then it must be here," Celeste told him. "I can't wait to see Beverly's face. Or yours," she added.

"Then do open them quickly," he urged. "They've been calling our flight since before you arrived."

Beverly started to untie the string carefully but Celeste, unable to contain her impatience, tore the string from the box with childish enthusiasm and lifted the lid, then stepped back to let Beverly discover the contents. Beverly unwrapped the tissue paper to find a rose-colored garment, and lifting it from the box, she saw it was one of the gowns she had admired at Couteau's shop. She looked from Celeste to André in bewilderment, then reached back into the box to find that it was filled with dozens of gowns.

"Do you like them?" Celeste demanded excitedly.

"I love them," she admitted, dazzled. "But when did you pack them? And how did you know my correct dress size?" She lifted a rasberry chiffon dress from the box and held it against her. She could tell in an instant that it was made to fit her.

"That is simple," André told her. "I have an eye for how women look, remember, and you are obviously the same size as our fashion models. I asked Colette, who gave you the tour, to keep track of the gowns you admired. While we were having our snack she had them boxed. I hope you like them."

"But I admired so many," Beverly protested.

"And I am pleased you thought so highly of my work," he said, accepting the compliment and returning it to her gracefully.

"Where will I wear them all?" Beverly wondered aloud.

"Sheldon will think of occasions appropriate to match the gowns," Celeste teased. "And not all work!"

"She won't have any trouble finding occasions to wear these gowns," he said indifferently, and again Beverly wondered what he meant. She rarely went out. She couldn't imagine wearing all these gowns in ten years. But she couldn't tell them that. There was no point upsetting them, and she did appreciate their gift. "I'm afraid we must hurry now," Sheldon said. "That was the final boarding call."

Beverly realized it was time to say good-bye to her new friends. She had known them such a short time, and already she felt a lifetime attachment to them. She hugged André warmly, and then Celeste. All three of them had tears in their eyes. Only Sheldon remained dry-eyed.

"You must come visit us soon," André stressed as Sheldon guided Beverly through the gateway.

"I will, I promise," Beverly called in return, using the silk handkerchief Celeste had given her to wipe the tears from her eyes.

"Before summer," Celeste added. "Even that is too long."

So much could happen in the next two months. A week before, Beverly had thought she would never survive a flight, and now she was agreeing to return, despite the plane ride.

She waved one last time. "Good-bye. I'll see you soon."

First class was more crowded this time. Beverly took her seat by the window, and Sheldon sat beside her. The stewardess had taken her packages, more for Sheldon's sake than for Beverly's. She started to thank him, but she saw his jaw was tense, and she hesitated to speak. Now that Beverly understood her feelings for him, his moodiness was even more difficult to tolerate.

She looked out the window, hoping to catch a final glimpse of Celeste and André, but her view was blocked by the wing. As the plane eased down the runway, she wondered at the calm she was experiencing. Miraculously, she wasn't frightened of the flight. Had the first flight, with all its trauma, erased her fear? Or was it having Sheldon beside her that calmed her? She thought back to the moonlit garden where she had first become aware of her feelings for Sheldon, to the peace she had felt inside Sainte-Chapelle, and knew these were the real reasons for her calm now. She might never admit her love for Sheldon to his face, and she might never experience his requited love, but she understood her feelings and felt better for admitting them—if only to herself.

Working with him would never be so easy again. The long hours he demanded would be complicated by the memory of his kiss. She would have to struggle every day to control her emotions, but she could do it. Clearly he had tired of her. He had taken his kiss and, seeing that he could have more, had wearied of the sport. Beverly's strategy had worked very well, she thought sadly. She remembered the woman she had seen him with in the hotel bar and forced herself to concentrate instead on the light from the cathedral's glass walls; they continued to shine, to quiet her misery, replacing it with an inner peace. Before the doubt could return, the stewardess was greeting them in English, welcoming them home to London.

chapter 7

AFTER THE UNREAL glow of Paris, London seemed dark and uninviting. Beverly watched the gray skies yield to rain as they rode from the airport into the dim city. By the time the car reached her house, she had to use the scarf Celeste had given her to cover her hair from the rain. The driver carried her luggage and the boxes of clothes to her fourth-floor flat while she stayed in the car. It took him several trips.

"So this is where you live," Sheldon remarked, surveying the old building with mild curiosity. He had said next to nothing during the long ride into town.

"Yes," she said proudly.

"Alone?" he dared.

"No. I share the flat with my friend Jancie," she offered. "I'd invite you up, but there's no telling what shape the place is in. Jancie's a dear, but housekeeping isn't her strong point."

Sheldon smiled. "I'll bet she depends on you to keep her in line," he said knowingly.

Beverly had to admit it. "You might say I'm the tidier

of the two." She was pretty sure Jancie would have straightened the house for her return, but she needed an excuse not to invite him up. She was tired and needed time alone to think about all that had happened in the last few days. "Would you mind terribly if I came in late tomorrow?" she asked hesitantly. "I'm dead tired, and I'll be up half the night unpacking." She didn't tell him that Jancie would insist on hearing about the trip in detail. It would be hours before she could go to sleep.

"Of course. If you weren't so essential in the office tomorrow, I'd give you the whole week off. You deserve it, Beverly, for signing the contract so fast, if nothing else. Someday you'll have to tell me how you did it." She started to tell him that she hadn't done anything, really, but he held up his hand in protest. "Why not come in at noon? But plan to stay late. I have volumes of work that need doing. And I'll bet Lizzie has left your office in the same shape your roommate has left your apartment." He smiled.

"I had forgotten about that," she admitted.

When the driver had finished unloading the car she said good night. Sheldon touched her shoulder so softly as she slid out that it made her quiver. She looked at him expectantly, but he didn't speak.

"Well, good night," she said again. "Thank you for introducing me to Paris."

"Did you enjoy yourself, Beverly?" he asked earnestly.

"I had a wonderful time," she told him dreamily. "Paris is even more perfect than I had imagined."

"I see," he said curtly. Again his mood had shifted. She couldn't keep up with him. "I'm glad you didn't feel compelled to work too hard," he added scornfully.

"No," she said, deciding to ignore his mood as best she could. "I enjoyed every minute of the time there." Except when you were with that woman, she thought. "I hope you enjoyed yourself too," she said. "You kept very long hours.

As usual." Suddenly all the warmth had disappeared between them.

"Except for a meeting or two, which you didn't attend, I hardly noticed I was working. I enjoy my work, Miss Milford. Always have."

"I'm sure you do. Most people wouldn't even call it work. But then we both know how much effort you put into your pursuits."

"Not too much effort," he said. "In some cases, there was no effort at all. Some people make work a pleasure. Surely you learned that in your 'work' with André."

"True. I did," she told him bitingly. "An ideal man to work with," she finished, before accepting the chauffeur's hand at last. She stepped out into the wet, dark night. "Good night," she said dryly.

"Right-o," he said briskly and pulled the door shut behind her.

Upstairs in the flat Beverly was glad for Jancie's predictable company. Beverly unpacked the new gowns as Jancie watched appreciatively. Her roommate assured her they would never go out of style, that the simple, elegant dresses would last a lifetime.

Seeing that Beverly was tired, Jancie excused herself early and went to her room. Jancie had told Beverly a little about the time she had spent with Julian, and Bev secretly envied the simple affection between them that was developing into love.

She felt somewhat foolish wearing the sheer nightgown from André's collection alone in her big bed. She hoped she would fall right to sleep, but hours later she was still awake, having thought of nothing but Sheldon. She wondered if he too were wakeful. She knew the unlikelihood of his being alone on his first night back in town. It was just a matter of whom he called first. Again she determined never to end up in his black book. It wouldn't satisfy the feelings she had for him, and it would humiliate her, force her to leave a job she not only loved but needed. She couldn't stop caring for him, but she didn't have to make a fool of herself in the process.

In the morning, despite the little sleep from the night before, Beverly awoke at her usual early hour. She cooked breakfast for herself and Jancie, and even after straightening the apartment, she found she was ready for work at nine o'clock. She took the bus instead of the underground train and reached the office at ten.

Sheldon had predicted correctly the mess in her office, and Beverly plunged right in straightening her desk. There was no one in sight, and she wondered vaguely when Sheldon would be in.

She had just begun to put things in some sort of order when the phone rang for the first time that morning. She answered it at once, but something was wrong with her phone. The party at the other end couldn't hear her at all; hastily, she went into Sheldon's office to switch the call to his phone. But before she could find out who was calling, she noticed she wasn't alone in the office. On the red leather sofa, Sheldon lay tangled in an embrace with Lizzie Sexton! The secretary made a feeble attempt to pull her skirt down over her knees. Sheldon drew away from her as if nothing had happened. No trace of embarrassment crossed his face as Lizzie excused herself from his office.

Beverly did her best to control the tremor in her voice. She spoke to the person on the other end of the line, promising to get in touch with him later in the day. She commended herself on her coolness as she hung up the phone, but when she turned to face Sheldon she couldn't remember what she had promised to do for the caller. She stared at him, making little attempt to conceal her mounting contempt.

She waited for him to say something, to offer some kind

of explanation, but he said nothing, as if waiting for her to speak. An arrogant smile was beginning to form. "If I had known you were going to be in early, I would have waited."

Beverly burned with anger. She couldn't have controlled her fury if she had wanted to. "Let me tell you one thing, Sheldon Whitney," she said hotly. "I do my best, never complain about the long hours or the unexpected meetings. But I am not here to assist you in *that* kind of work. You can fire me if you wish, but I will *never*"—she paused to emphasize her point—"never allow you to touch me like that!"

"Come off your high horse, Bev," he said smugly. "I seem to remember you enjoyed yourself the day before we left for France. And don't forget the plane. Don't waste your time denying it. I wouldn't believe you if you tried."

"I don't care what you believe, or what you choose to think," she told him, collecting her nerve to tell him what she herself had been thinking all along. "The simple truth is that I *despise* your playboy mentality, and I refuse to participate in it." His smug expression told her he was not convinced, and she needed to settle this issue once and for all. It was now or never. "I thought nothing of your kiss," she went on, "and you're only fooling yourself if you think I did. I felt nothing! I only responded as I did because I feared losing my job. And now I don't care about my job enough to let you touch me ever again. Do you understand?"

"No," he told her fiercely. "You'll never convince me that you didn't feel anything when I kissed you. I could feel every fiber of your body wanting more. Why, you even looked disappointed when I insisted we put business first. Admit your true feelings. We live in the twentieth century, for God's sake."

"Why should I admit anything to you? So you can put another notch in your belt? You'll never conquer this one," she said, gesturing to herself. "I believe in love, and I don't hunger for anyone enough to want sex without it."

"Do you love your British boyfriend?" he asked spitefully. Beverly didn't answer; his question puzzled her into silence. "I see," he said. "I guess he'll take care of all your desires. Does he know how you respond to my kisses? Does he know you would have surrendered to—"

"Stop it!" Beverly screamed. "Don't ever talk to me that way again. You have no right!"

"You have no right to pretend you're indifferent to me. I'm tired of your voice quivering with indignation each time I express interest in a woman. I know you want me as much as I want you."

"You are forcing me to quit this job," she said boldly. "Would you like my resignation in writing?" She was surprised by her words. She hadn't meant to quit the job she loved so much, but the situation had gotten out of hand. There was no way she could retract her words. Besides, to a degree he was right. She did desire him. But she had never been casual with her sexual favors. When she had married Larry she was a virgin, and except for the month of their marriage she had never slept with a man. She retained the ideal that sex was a beautiful expression of love, to be given to the man who shared that dream. Sheldon's casual affairs were a travesty of the life she believed in. She resented his promiscuity. How dare he accuse her of sharing his miserable standards of behavior?

They had gone too far, had said too much to restore the civility between them. "I'll stay on the job until you've found someone to replace me," she said. "Someone who is more obliging, perhaps," she added bitingly, before leaving the office for her own.

The rest of the day was miserable for her. She had no idea what she would do with her life. She loved her job, the demands of working for such a talented man. She knew she would never find another job that would satisfy her as this one had. She could go back to New York and work for her former boss, Douglas Whitney, but she didn't think she could face returning to New York. Yet she had no choice but to leave. Her pride would never allow her to ask to stay on, even if she thought Sheldon would consider it.

Sheldon avoided her all day. At five o'clock, when she couldn't think of an excuse to stay any longer, she left the office with all the other secretaries. Not since the first day of her job had she gone home so early.

When she arrived at work the next morning she found that all of Lizzie's belongings had been removed. The office was neat and orderly. Fresh flowers filled two vases. All ready for someone to move in, Beverly thought. They don't waste much time.

Sheldon didn't appear until after one o'clock, and when she saw him he looked as miserable as she felt. He seemed to have slept as badly as she had. Was he, too, sorry that she was leaving the firm? As much as she wanted to, she couldn't ask.

They did their best to avoid each other for the remainder of the day. When it was essential for them to discuss business, they were polite, reserved, as brief as possible.

At five o'clock Beverly knocked on Sheldon's door. His face was drawn and tired, the usual vitality gone. Beverly wondered if he was well.

"If there's nothing else for me to do today, Mr. Whitney, I'll go home now," she told him. She kept her concern from her voice, but her hand jerked at her side as she restrained herself from touching his forehead to check for a temperature.

"Just one thing," he said wearily. "I don't want you to quit." He looked her straight in the eye, and she thought her heart would stop. "I won't say I'm sorry," he said quickly. "And I don't insist that you apologize either. But

you are the best secretary I've ever had, and I need you—
I need you to work with me." Before Beverly could speak
he raised his hand to stop her. "I know you don't want to
stay. But I hope you'll listen and reconsider. I will never
again make an advance, I promise. I was misled. I did think
you were interested in more than a working relationship.
Now that I know you're not, I'll keep clear of you. Your
private life will remain private, and I'll do what I can to
keep mine away from the office. Will you think about staying on? You don't have to answer right away. Take the
evening, but please..." His eyes were dark and uncertain.
"Please, do think about it. I need you."

Beverly nodded. She hurried back to her office and sank
into her chair. Tears brimmed in her eyes, and she knew
she had to find solitude in which to think about all he had
said. Hastily she gathered her purse and coat and ran to the
elevator, catching it before it descended.

chapter 8

"BUT HOW CAN I go back after all we've said to each other?"
Jancie sat at the edge of Beverly's bed. They had been
talking for hours and were still at the same point.

"Didn't you say he *asked* you to come back?"

"Yes," she admitted guardedly. She didn't know what
she thought, and she didn't want Jancie to decide for her.

"I can imagine what that cost him, with *his* male pride.
Doesn't that count for anything?"

"I guess so. But still—"

"Listen," Jancie said softly. "Are you in love with the
man?"

Beverly looked at her in astonishment. Were her senti-
ments so visible? "Why do you ask that?"

"Because I think that's the real issue. Well, are you?"

"Is it that clear?" Beverly asked.

"I'm afraid so."

"Do you think he knows?"

"It doesn't sound like he does," Jancie speculated. "Do
you want to keep the job?"

"Yes!"

"Then *that's* settled! Tell him you'll stay."

"You think I should?" Beverly repeated. She needed to hear Jancie's advice again.

"Yes," Jancie said quietly. "But it is *you* who have to decide. As for me, I have to be at work very early tomorrow morning."

"I'm sorry to keep you awake," Beverly apologized.

"Don't start fretting about that. I've kept you awake plenty. Besides, your problem has put my own into perspective. I was feeling the weight of the world on my shoulders until I heard your worries. Now I feel easier."

"What's been bothering you?" Beverly asked tenderly. "Here I've been keeping you up all night, and you never let me know you were troubled."

"Well," Jancie confided, resuming her place on the edge of Beverly's bed, "Julian is getting serious, and I have to decide if I want to spend the rest of my life with him."

"You mean he's asked you to marry him?" Beverly asked incredulously, leaning forward on her knees. She hadn't thought their affections had grown to this point, but she was learning that the world was full of surprises. She grabbed Jancie's hand in excitement.

Jancie smiled at her shyly. "You might say he proposed a life together." She giggled. "He's so shy that I didn't gather his drift—I had to ask him if he was proposing marriage, and then he blushed so deeply I was sorry I had spoken. When will I learn to keep my mouth shut?"

"But what did he say?" Beverly pressed joyfully. "And when did he ask you? And why didn't you tell me at once? Here I've been droning on about my problems and taking the limelight from you. How could you let me?"

"I knew there would be time to tell you. And besides, listening to your questions about Sheldon Whitney gave me time to think about how I really feel about Julian."

"And how do you feel about him? Do you love him?"

"That's just it. I don't know for sure."

"But that's ridiculous. When you love someone, it's as bright as day. Bells ring and lights flash. How can you not know for sure?"

"There are lots of kinds of love, remember? I don't love Julian if I measure it in flashing lights and screaming sirens." She looked serious as she spoke. "But I *care* for Julian, and he cares for me. He would make a good husband and a wonderful father to our children."

"But won't you miss the drama, the passion? I understand what you say about the caring, but is that enough?"

Jancie had to laugh. "If you could hear yourself. These are the questions I've been asking *you* all along. Remember how you said you didn't want to be taken into orbit, you wanted warmth but not fire? Now listen to you."

Beverly was silent. Was she being a fool to prescribe passion, or was Jancie settling for a lukewarm affair because she was afraid of more? It was hard to tell. "There is no telling, is there," she conceded. "When I was married to Larry, I thought I had it all. I was very happy, and calm. Now"—her eyes dampened—"now, all I feel is confusion and desire. You're right to be happy with Julian. He's kind, and he's good to you."

"He is," Jancie said quietly. "And I think he will make me very happy. But not everyone is happy with mild-mannered affection. Once you've tasted the kind of passion you describe, it may be impossible to settle for anything less."

Beverly nodded solemnly. "Like Eve, having tasted the forbidden fruit."

"Exactly," Jancie punctuated. "But the garden, however perfect, was without the sweet agony of love. Would you trade Sheldon for Julian? That's what you have to ask yourself. That's what I have to ask myself. It would be unfair for either of us to commit ourselves to either man until we're certain."

"Certain is the only thing I'm not! Besides, we're talking about two different worlds. Julian's asked you to spend your life with him. All Sheldon's asked is that I continue to work for him. He loves my secretarial skills." She swallowed hard. "He's even promised to restrict his attentions to work. I'll never have to worry about kissing him again. I have his word of honor. Oh, if he only knew!"

"There's one way he'd know for sure," Jancie offered. Beverly looked up from the bedspread directly into her friend's eyes. "You could tell him."

"I could never do that! What if he laughed at me? Worse, what if he used me! He could make my life miserable."

"More miserable than you are now? We aren't talking about your *attraction*. We're talking about your deepest feelings. Your love. He should know you well enough to know you wouldn't speak lightly of your affections. Don't you think?"

"I just don't know what to think. All I know is that I love him and I wish I didn't." Beverly groaned.

Jancie grinned as she stood to leave. "Well, he'll never love you if you come to work with dark circles under your eyes."

Beverly brightened. "Maybe I can wear the black dress André gave me. Maybe then he'll look at me with interest."

"As far as I can tell, that's not the problem. It's his love you want, not his roving eye, remember?" Beverly nodded quickly. "All you have to do is make sure you don't force him away. Sometimes, darling, you do build roadblocks when clear roads might better serve you. Now not another word. To sleep!" she ordered before closing the door behind her gently.

The next morning, long before Beverly heard any stirrings from Jancie's room, she was awake and planning her day. She turned the heat up on her way to the bathroom, but she noticed the apartment wasn't as chilly as she expected it to be. It was only six o'clock, but the day was already bright. Soon summer would be here, and they could open the apartment windows, put away the heavy rugs on the floors, and spend evenings out of doors, enjoying the extended daylight.

It was hard to be unhappy on such a beautiful day. She thought back to her uncertainty of the night before. Just as night had passed into daylight, her gloom had passed into cheer. Not that she knew what she was going to do about her feelings for Sheldon, but she felt less urgent somehow. She had awakened remembering a dream, a happy memory of her first days at Whitney-Forbes, the first time she had met Sheldon. She took the dream as a sign that everything would be all right.

Outside, the sun was warm on her shoulders, the sky a light shade of blue; there was not a cloud in sight. The streets were beginning to fill when she rounded the corner of Bond Street. She smiled pleasantly as she passed a few familiar faces. At the flower stall, she greeted her friend with her usual smile, but he didn't smile back. "What's wrong?" she asked, stopping to talk with him for the first time. "Is something the matter?"

"Oh, hullo, miss. No, nothing is wrong. Just that today is my last day. I'm retiring, you know. I was filled with the glory of the day, dreaming of my retirement, until I saw you and remembered that leaving my job meant no longer greeting you these early mornings."

"Why, that's wonderful news. And you shan't miss me at all. I'll think of you each day, just when I would be passing by here. And you'll know it too, won't you?"

The old man's face lit up. "Will you, miss? Will you remember me when I'm gone?"

"Of course," she assured him, and leaned to kiss his smooth pink cheek. "Where are you retiring to?"

"Me and the missus are moving to Nottingham. To be near our youngest girl and her babies. The missus wants to spend her days feeling the sun on her face, near her young grandchildren."

"That sounds wonderful. How can we be sad with such good news? I will miss you," Beverly told him truthfully. "But I am very happy for you." She accepted the long-stemmed rose from him for the final time and bowed gratefully before hurrying on to work. So many changes so quickly. Thank goodness she was in high spirits.

It was early when she got to the office, not yet seven. She would have time to look through the work she had been too disheartened to consider the day before.

The sun was bright in her office. She settled into work at once. When the phone rang an hour later, she answered it cheerfully, absorbed in the duties of her job. When she hung up—the printer had called to inquire about the order she had placed last week—she was surprised to find Sheldon watching her from the other side of the room.

"Oh," she said, startled. "I didn't hear you come in."

"You were humming to yourself. May I ask what you're so happy about?" He stood in front of her desk, a curious grin on his handsome face.

"It's hard to be anything but ecstatic on a day like today! Besides, I have a job which I love, and a very capable employer. What more could a girl ask for?" She smiled, and her face glowed with joy.

"That means you'll stay?" he asked cautiously.

"If you'll have me," she told him.

He leaned over her desk and touched her arm affectionately. "Thank you, Miss Milford. I had hoped you would agree. You won't be sorry," he promised her. "I have some news which I think you'll like to hear. Guess who's in town?" He glanced at the wide dial of his gold watch. "In about an hour, that is?"

"Who?" she asked jubilantly.

"Our boss," Sheldon said. Beverly looked at him questioningly. "My father," he explained.

"How wonderful!" Beverly cried. She hadn't seen the senior Mr. Whitney since she left the States, and she had a soft spot for the elderly gentleman. "What brings him to London?"

"Guess he wants to make sure we're doing our job. You know, check the stock supplies to make sure we're buying the right size rubber bands, that sort of thing." His dark eyes sparkled. Beverly was elated by his good mood. "Actually," he said, no longer teasing, "he is worried about the sugar contract. It's a very big deal, and he wants to insure that the account isn't jeopardized by lack of thought. Which is to say, he wants to put in his two cents' worth, in case we haven't covered all the angles."

"Not a chance of that," she said confidently. "Not the way your mind works."

Sheldon nodded at the compliment. "Just an excuse to visit London, if you ask me."

"Are you meeting him at the airport?"

"I hadn't planned to, but now that you mention it, that's a good idea. I was just going to send the car for him." He hesitated for a minute. "Would you like to come along? He'd get a kick out of seeing you first off. We can spend the hour drive planning our line of action for the sugar campaign."

Beverly beamed at his idea. She glanced at her desk. There was nothing that couldn't wait a few hours. "I'd love to. Let me put these papers in order. I'll be ready in five, all right?"

"Great. Bring your note pad. I'll have important things to say."

"Of course," she said, grinning unrestrainedly at his playful arrogance. Oh, she had been right to stay at the job.

What a difference it was, now that the air was cleared. They could be friendly with one another, which was exactly what Beverly wanted, without the risk of losing herself to his promiscuity. Her only sadness was that they hadn't cleared the air before they went to Paris. But there was no use wishing for what hadn't been. Onward. Forward. To tomorrow, she thought happily, picking up her note pad and putting on her coat.

They worked diligently all the way to the airport and arrived just as the plane delivered Douglas Whitney from America.

Beverly greeted the old man with renewed fondness. He was particularly delighted to see her and voiced his appreciation at being met at the airport.

On the outskirts of the city they stopped for breakfast. Beverly wasn't hungry and neither was Sheldon, but Mr. Whitney insisted that he hadn't been able to eat on the plane.

Sheldon ordered coffee and rolls for Beverly and himself and an English breakfast for his father. "Now confess," Sheldon teased. "You just wanted to taste English cooking."

"You know your old man well," Douglas agreed. "I can do without British cooking most of the time, but I do miss the big breakfast. Never have been able to adjust to coffee and toast, the way most Americans do." He took a bite of the stewed tomatoes and rolled his eyes upward appreciatively. "Now tell me, what have you thought about this sugar crisis?"

Beverly watched him for a moment. "I don't understand—why is it a crisis?" she asked. "I mean, isn't it just another large account? And Lord knows we have handled larger."

"There is one problem you don't realize in London. In America there is a wave of fanaticism about sugar. Sugar blues. Health kicks. People are using honey, or molasses, of all things—goodness knows how they can prefer that sticky stuff—or doing without sugar altogether. They have the idea that sugar is unhealthy. And the manufacturers—don't get me wrong, they don't want us to lie to the public, but they don't want to suffer from this health-food over-reaction. How can we show that sugar has its place in the well-balanced diet?"

"Why not show it in its natural form," Beverly offered. "You could show Hawaiian kids chewing on sugar cane. Or a tanned young man carrying his surfboard stopping on his way back from the beach to pick a stock of cane for quick energy."

Sheldon stared at her in disbelief. "Did I say something wrong?" Beverly asked.

"Not on your life," Sheldon assured her.

"Where did you find this young lady?" Mr. Whitney said. "Or, I should ask, how did I ever let her out of my sight? No wonder the London firm does so well. Is she always this brilliant?"

"At least," he said, beaming at Beverly.

Beverly looked at them in disbelief. "What did I say?" she asked. Why were they staring at her like that, and why was Sheldon grinning from ear to ear?

"I might as well get right back on that plane," Douglas Whitney said. "In fact, I might as well resign and give the presidency over to you, young lady. How'd you get to be so smart?"

"It was just an idea," Beverly said.

"And a terrific one. Problem solved! Say, how would you like to return with me to New York?" His kind old eyes twinkled.

"Don't get any ideas about stealing her from me," Sheldon told his father. "She's mine. You had your chance."

"Don't worry," Mr. Whitney said, taking Beverly's hand into his own. "I see she is best off with you." He stroked her hand and smiled warmly. "You were a promising bud when you left New York," he told her, "but you have blossomed in London."

"You two make me feel like royalty."

"That is how you make me feel," Sheldon told her, and she thought she saw him redden under his tanned complexion.

She brushed a wisp of hair from her eyes. "Shall we go?" she suggested when she saw Mr. Whitney had finished. In a minute they had paid the bill and returned to the car. Soon they were back at the office.

Sheldon asked Beverly to conduct his father around the office while he ran over his notes for the board meeting that afternoon at three. When she and Mr. Whitney returned she found him a comfortable chair in her office and made a fresh pot of tea for the two of them.

"Are you happy?" he asked her confidentially when the tea was brewed.

"Very," she told him truthfully.

"You look wonderful," he told her. "Your dress is most becoming."

"One of our new accounts," she said and told him about André's gift, the boxes of clothes.

"I see I wasn't overstating the effect you've had on the business for the firm," he remarked. "Does Sheldon give you credit for your accomplishments?"

"It's nothing, really," Beverly insisted. "It's he who does it all. I'm just there to take some of the credit. He does all the hard work."

"Don't sell yourself short," he told her. "Looks like you run this place." Again his eyes twinkled. "Do you enjoy working with my son?"

"Oh, yes," she said enthusiastically, "he's wonderful to work for. Always full of good ideas, good—"

"Are you in love with him?" he interrupted. Beverly blushed crimson before she could stop herself.

"I thought so. Does he know it?" he asked.

Beverly shook her head ashamedly. "No." Soon everyone in the world would know, she thought desperately, except for Sheldon.

"And you don't dare tell him, do you?" the old man guessed. Again Beverly nodded her head. "You could be in love with worse, if you don't mind my bragging. Sheldon has his faults—plenty of them—but he also has his attributes. I've always puzzled why he hasn't settled down yet. Any ideas?"

Beverly wanted to tell him that she thought he liked variety too much to settle for the confines of marriage, but she didn't dare. Perhaps his father didn't know of his son's reputation. "Maybe he just hasn't fallen in love with anyone yet," she offered, looking away from his clear gaze.

"Oh, I wouldn't be surprised if he had," the old man speculated. Beverly looked at him, not understanding. "Give him time. Don't turn him away too fast," he instructed. "As I said, he's rough in some spots, and one of them is courtship, but he's a diamond underneath."

Beverly couldn't believe her ears. Clearly Mr. Whitney *didn't* know his son's reputation with women. Untutored in courtship! There was none smoother, Beverly thought scornfully, but she concealed her thoughts.

"Sheldon's mother was a real lady," Douglas Whitney reminisced. "And while she was alive, she spoiled Sheldon rotten. Gave him everything he wanted. He never learned how to ask for what he wants, and in some cases, he would rather do without than risk rejection."

Beverly wondered if they were talking about the same person. Sheldon Whitney knew exactly what he wanted and had no trouble asking, or taking. As if reading her thoughts, Douglas Whitney continued, "Of course, he's more comfortable asking for the less important things. But when it comes to serious courtship, I think he's got to be reassured like the rest of us." He paused to sip his tea. "He's keen on you, Bev. Don't let his roughness fool you. Give him a chance. I would be pleased to have you in the family, and I'd be relieved to see Sheldon settle down. It's about time. Besides, I want at least one grandchild before my time is up."

Beverly was thinking of what to say when Sheldon joined them. "Are you bending her ear, Father?" he said playfully. He poured himself a cup of tea and sat on the arm of the chair beside his father.

Beverly wondered at the difference between the two men. Sheldon was taller than his father by several inches. His hair showed the first hints of silver, while Mr. Whitney's hair was entirely gray; there was not a touch of the original black Beverly remembered from working with him in New York. Lines of laughter surrounded Mr. Whitney's dark eyes, though there was the same dangerous spark in them that Sheldon had.

Both men dressed with extreme care, though Sheldon's clothes were more dashing, less conservative. Douglas Whitney had acquired a few extra pounds since Beverly last saw him, but they were becoming to his age. Sheldon, on the other hand, was as fit, as slim, as his father had no doubt been in the prime of his life. Sheldon's features were as vital as the first day of spring, and Beverly regretfully noticed that Mr. Whitney looked tired and worn, especially around the mouth. Beverly dreaded the idea of Sheldon getting tired. More than anything she wanted to watch him grow old painlessly.

Beverly's idea was accepted unanimously by the members of the board that afternoon, and Sheldon embarrassed her by giving her too much credit. They worked out the basic details and left the rest for the advertising staff to consider. Everyone agreed that Sheldon should accompany the crew to Hawaii, where the series of commercials would be shot. It was to be the biggest commercial effort Whitney-

Forbes had contracted to date, and Beverly swelled with pride at the manner in which Sheldon handled the discussion.

Sheldon invited Beverly to join him and his father for supper, but Beverly wanted to transcribe the notes from the meeting before morning, when Mr. Whitney would return to New York. Douglas started to insist that she join them, but Sheldon stepped in. "If she doesn't want to come along, Father, that's a decision we must respect, in spite of our wishes to the contrary." He nodded pleasantly at Beverly. "It's the condition of our working relationship," he explained to his father.

"Then let me say good-bye, Beverly," Mr. Whitney said grandly, opening his arms in a gentlemanly gesture. Beverly accepted his embrace, noticing the difference between Mr. Whitney's reserve and his son's intensity. "I would love to convince you to return with me," he said gallantly, "but I see you have made London your home. Do you miss us at all?"

Beverly nodded earnestly, and hugged the old man, assuring him of her genuine liking and respect of him. "Do see that Sheldon treats you well," he said in parting.

"If I didn't know my father so well," Sheldon remarked, "I'd say he had an eye for you."

"Where do you think you inherit your good taste?" the old man retorted.

After they had left, Beverly got down to her work. She called Jancie to tell her she would be late coming home.

"That's all right," Jancie said. "I burned the dinner so badly that Julian and I decided to go out. We'll see you after dinner, if you're not too late. Julian's got to be home early. Court tomorrow, and all."

Beverly had finished the notes and was duplicating them when Sheldon returned. "Still here?" he asked. "I'm sorry to see you working so hard, but I have to admit I'm secretly glad to find you here."

"I've just finished," she said.

"Quite a day we've had," Sheldon commented, taking a cigarette and a gold lighter from his coat pocket. "You should be proud of yourself. Dad is as impressed as I am."

Beverly beamed at him gratefully. "I'm pleased that everything worked out so well, too. When you told me your father was coming over, I began to worry that we really would have a product we couldn't manage. But I guess sugar is as sweet a product for Whitney-Forbes as any."

"All because of you, of course."

"You are too kind."

"On the contrary, I'm just giving you the credit you deserve. Thank you, Beverly." He paused, as if to say something more. "And thank you for staying on with the job. I know I can be impossible at times. No one else would put up with me. I would have dreaded coming to the office tomorrow if you had decided to quit."

"I'm glad I stayed too," she said softly. She toyed with the pen on her desk, not daring to look up. "Well, I guess that about does it for today," she said at last.

"A long day, and a job well done. Can I offer you a lift home? The car is parked below. Your house is on the way."

"Are you sure it's no trouble?"

"It's the least I can do, to thank you for your help. Are you nearly ready?" he asked.

"Yes, the rest of this can wait until morning. I have your father's copy here. Can we stop by his hotel on the way home? I had planned to deliver it in the morning, but this way he'll have time to read it before he leaves."

"Good thinking. Of course."

Beverly collected her belongings while Sheldon disappeared into his office. She longed for a mindless soak in a hot tub. As it was, she would have to visit with Jancie and Julian before she could remove her clothes and forget about her manners.

"Ready?" Sheldon queried. He was toting his briefcase, and Beverly imagined he would be up half the night working. She admired his devotion.

"When you are," she quipped, accepting his arm and joining him as they walked to the elevator.

They stopped briefly at the hotel to drop off the notes Beverly had transcribed. Douglas thanked her again, and insisted that he could see himself to the airport in the morning. His eyes twinkled wickedly, and Beverly knew he was hoping she was going home with Sheldon now. They were more alike than she had thought, she realized as they said good-bye for the last time.

It was just after midnight when the limousine reached Beverly's apartment. She was so tired she could hardly think straight, but the exhaustion felt good, like a long climb to the top of a mountain, legs tired, but the view so magnificent that one didn't care about aching muscles.

Sheldon helped her out of the car and walked her to her apartment.

"Beverly," he said softly, when they reached the door. She wondered if he would try to kiss her or ask to come up. The day had been so perfect, he might think she would want him to. She waited expectantly, not knowing how she would respond. "Would you consider accompanying me to. Hawaii for the shoot next week?"

"Can I let you know tomorrow?" she answered. She had to consider carefully.

"Of course. I assumed you would have people to confer with," he said.

"Mostly it depends on the pile of work on my desk," she said. "I still have so much to do from before our Paris trip," she reminded him. "And if I'm going to deserve the credit you and your father insist on bestowing on me, I must tackle that pile of unfinished business."

"Surely someone else can do it while you're gone."

"To be truthful," Beverly told him, "when we were in Paris the work seemed to double, not disappear." Beverly had wondered if Lizzie had done anything other than file her nails and eat chocolates. "But I'll know better tomorrow. Another day like today and I'll feel like I can manage anything in the entire world."

"Which I'm sure you can," Sheldon said.

She looked at him shyly. "No," she said thoughtfully. "Not everything." Not you, she thought privately.

"I'm sure if you put your mind to it, you can do just about anything you please."

They studied each other before Beverly broke the silence. "I'll let you know in the morning. Do you know when you'll be in?" she asked.

"In time for your answer," he said at once, then reconsidered. "About eleven. Despite Father's protests, I think I'll take him to the airport. He won't admit it, but he does like to be fussed over. Want to come along?" he asked hopefully.

"Not if you want me to come along to Hawaii," she said. "Oh," she thought suddenly. "I suppose we would be flying?"

"Is there any other choice!" he asked.

"I thought not. Well, good night," she said softly. "I'll see you tomorrow."

He lifted her hand and brushed it gently with his lips. "Thank you again, Beverly," he said tenderly before releasing her hand.

True to his word, he didn't try anything further. He waited until she was safely inside the front door before returning to the car. By the time Beverly reached the door to her flat the limousine was out of sight, leaving the street deserted, the night quiet.

chapter 9

THERE WERE SO many details to attend to during the week
before their departure that Beverly saw little of Jancie. They
exchanged pleasantries in the mornings, before Beverly left
for work, and in the moment or two before bed, if Jancie
was still awake when Beverly finally arrived home. She was
working harder than usual, but she didn't mind. Her job
was as she remembered it before Sheldon's disposition had
soured. Once again he was gracious and considerate of her,
and she basked in her good fortune, hoping it would last
forever.

She wasn't alone in her hard work. Sheldon kept equally
long hours, often surprising her by arriving at work before
she did, no matter how early she managed to arrive. He
continued the courtesy of delivering her to her doorstep each
evening, using the time to review the progress they had
made during the day. And always at the door he took her
hand in his, in gratitude for the day well spent, but he never
tried to kiss her, and he never suggested he wanted more
from her than her earnest efforts on the job.

Gradually she came to accept his behavior as routine,

and the last threads of her defensiveness dissolved. By the end of the week, two days before they were to leave for Hawaii, she was laughing with him as easily as she did with Jancie.

Friday evening, after the rest of the employees had left the office to go home to their families and weekend plans, Sheldon joined Beverly in her office and collapsed dramatically in the chair facing her desk. "What a week!" he remarked triumphantly. "At this rate we will have the world conquered in less than a month."

Beverly put aside the papers she had been studying. "I doubt it would take nearly that long, with you at the helm." She smiled confidently. "I even think I'll be ready for Hawaii on Monday with just a few more hours work tomorrow," she assured him. "That is, unless you've come in here with *more* work for me to do before Monday," she added suspiciously.

"Not on your life. I've taken care of all the plans for filming and I'm sure you've covered every angle of your responsibilities—"

"Models, wardrobe, agents, passports." Beverly ran down the list in front of her. "I'm glad we're arriving before the others, however, because I'm sure there will be things to tend to there. Can you think of anything else?"

"Nope. Not a thing. In fact, the reason I've come in here is to insist you stay away from the office all weekend."

"But I have at least—"

"On pain of death!" he insisted, rising up in his chair before falling back in a slump. "Even God rested, for heaven's sake. And I want you to be rested for this trip. You'll need all your strength once we get there."

"Yes, sir!" Beverly saluted. "Anything else?"

"Yes. I want you to let me take you to dinner now. It's time to quit."

Beverly shook her head. "You can't have it both ways,"

she said. Sheldon looked at her questioningly. "Either I stay away all weekend, or I work late tonight. Really, I must finish this schedule tonight, or we'll arrive in Honolulu disorganized."

Sheldon threw up his hands in defeat. "All right, you run this place," he said agreeably. "Come to think of it, I have some work to do, too. But what about a dinner break? I'm famished, and you have to eat something."

"I have a better idea," she proposed. "Why don't I call out for fish and chips. We can eat here and finish work quickly so we can both get home earlier. And I'll take a rain check on the dinner invite until we're in Hawaii, all right?"

The idea seemed to appeal to him. "Right!" he agreed. His vitality returned. "What a slave driver I've got for a boss." he said. "But order me steak and chips, will you?"

"Whatever you say," Beverly answered, reaching for the phone.

Sheldon gathered himself up and returned to his office. They worked diligently until dinner arrived. Even then they ate hurriedly, preferring to get on with the work. In less than three hours, Beverly had finished the stack of work on top of her desk. What remained could wait until she returned the following week. The important matters were cleared up.

She thought ahead to the countless personal details she had to attend to before she was ready to leave for the islands. She needed casual clothes and a bathing suit. She was determined to find time to visit the beaches in between business commitments.

She flipped through the pile of work—contracts, forms, announcements—that she would have to take with her and put it in her attaché case. Everything was in order: the plants were watered; notes for Eileen, who would replace her during the week, completed; unfinished business locked away securely.

When she was certain she hadn't forgotten anything she knocked on Sheldon's door. He, too, was just finishing up, and she sat in the plush chair in his office, watching him while he finished. In minutes he was through; together they locked the doors to the suite of offices and took the lift to the lobby of the building.

"As much as I like this place," Beverly said as they walked to the car, "I'm glad for the chance to go away for a while."

Sheldon held the car door open for her. "You do like working here, don't you, Bev?" His question was genuine, and she could tell he was glad she enjoyed her work.

"Very much," she said enthusiastically. "And," she added, "I'm going to love Hawaii, once we're there."

"Are you dreading the flight?"

"Not quite so much after reaching Paris safely," she admitted. "But crossing over the first time, I was terrified."

"Why are you so anxious about flying?" he asked. "A bad experience?"

"You might say that," she answered vaguely. "But I'm going to relish those white sandy beaches," she said, hoping to turn his attention from her to their travels.

"Be sure to bring a swimsuit," he advised.

"I plan to. Do you think we'll have time, really, to enjoy the sights?"

"If I have anything to say about it we will. I hear the restaurants are first-rate."

"Better than fish and chips?" she teased.

"Let's hope so!"

They rode through the London streets in silence, enjoying the quiet satisfaction of well-spent energy until they reached Beverly's house. "You'll have to invite me up sometime," he said, "now that I pose no threat to you."

"I'd be happy to," she told him sincerely. "When I've given Jancie fair warning—so she won't be caught in a mess."

Sheldon laughed. "That bad, really?"

"Worse!"

They shared a vision of chaos awaiting Beverly upstairs as he walked her to her door. He would send a car for her Monday morning. Their plane left at eight o'clock. There would be no time to return to the office before they left, he reminded her. "And if I hear you've done a shred of work over the weekend, I'll make you pay for our dinner in Hawaii. And I plan to run up quite a bill."

Beverly promised, her hand held high in oath. "I'll see you Monday morning," she said softly before turning to run up the four flights of stairs to her flat.

"Try to rest if you can," Sheldon instructed after the plane had reached altitude. The stewardess had brought her a pillow and a small blanket. "It's a long flight, as you know. And because of the time difference, it will be only midday when we reach Honolulu. And knowing you, you'll feel compelled to put in a full day's work."

Beverly thought about the twelve-hour flight to Los Angeles, the two-hour layover, the five-hour balance of flying time to Hawaii.

"I had forgotten about the layover until this minute," Beverly said. She had held her breath during takeoff and had managed to calm her nerves, but she didn't look forward to another landing and takeoff before reaching Hawaii. "But I imagine it's only civilized, if we're expected ever to walk again." She stretched her legs out in front of her. "Think of the poor souls in the rear of the plane."

Sheldon shook his head gravely. "I try not to," he said. "Now rest up." He adjusted the pillow beneath her head, then picked up the magazine from the pocket in front of him.

Beverly closed her eyes, but she knew she would never sleep. Not as long as they were in the air. How she envied those people who could walk up and down the aisle without a thought to their safety. Or the stewardess! But they had no reason to be afraid. She *knew* how fatal flying could be. It had taken her husband from her, and that wasn't a lesson she would ever forget, no matter how many safe flights tried to persuade her otherwise. The plane engine hummed in her ears. She could feel the vibrations of the aircraft through every pore of her body. Thank goodness Sheldon was beside her.

After a while she convinced him she wasn't tired and relaxed into the book she had brought to read during the trip. It had a good strong plot, and soon she was engrossed in the lives of the characters. She had just reached the last chapter when the stewardess announced their arrival in Los Angeles. Before she had time to worry the plane had landed, and Sheldon was ushering her out of the terminal, into the center of the airport, and up an escalator to a restaurant perched high atop a modern, spacelike structure.

They enjoyed a leisurely brunch. Sheldon promised that when they stopped in Los Angeles on their return trip he would take her to a wonderful Mexican restaurant he had discovered on his last trip west. "It's so tiny," he told her, "that twelve people fill the entire place."

"How can it stay in business?" Beverly asked.

"Because they serve the best *burritos* this side of Guatemala," he pronounced. "And there are always a dozen hungry patrons waiting outside, ready to pounce on the first empty seat. They don't have a liquor license, but everyone brings their own beer. And the owners don't worry about people taking an hour to eat or loitering after they've finished," he continued. "Because the food's so good, it's hard to eat it slowly, and the setting is so offensive no one wants to hang around afterward."

"It sounds perfectly horrid," Beverly said with a giggle. "And I would love to try it." She glanced around at the plush setting of the airport restaurant, high above the traffic and noise. Planes buzzed all around them, arriving from and departing to places unknown. Beverly was amazed by her calm. Six months before she would have been terrified just to sit and watch a plane take off. And here she was, finishing her meal while waiting to board a plane for the second time in one day.

"Shall we be going?" Sheldon asked when they had finished eating. "We still have thirty minutes, if you care to tour the airport."

"I would like to walk a bit."

"Me too," he said, signaling the waiter.

They made the entire circuit of the airport and reached their terminal just minutes before the stewardess had advised them to return. They took their seats, and the plane returned smoothly to the sky. This time Beverly was less anxious than before. She knew that by the time they landed in Hawaii her fear of flying would have been cured. Her loss would stay with her for the rest of her life, but she would be free of the symptoms that had kept her landlocked until now.

To her surprise Beverly did nap finally. She woke with a start, her hearing partially blocked. "We're landing," Sheldon told her. "I was just about to wake you. Swallow hard," he instructed, and as soon as she did her hearing was restored.

She looked out her window and saw a cluster of tall buildings. "Oh!" Beverly exclaimed, her voice edged with disappointment. "I had expected a small village. Why, this could be any downtown metropolis."

"Yes," Sheldon agreed. "But you'll feel the difference once we're on the ground. Right outside the city are the most spectacular beaches and lava mountains you've ever seen. And an hour outside of Honolulu you'll never remember that the city exists."

Beverly beamed. "Can we at least look at the beach today?" she asked hopefully.

"We can do better than that," he said fervently. "I was afraid you were going to insist we get straight to work upon arrival. Let's check our bags into the hotel and grab a car. We'll spend the rest of the day looking at beaches and not think about work until tomorrow, all right?"

"Do you think we dare?" she asked skeptically. She thought of the hours of preparation she had to put in before the crews arrived.

"I doubt the boss will find out," he quipped. "Unless you plan on telling. Besides," he told her earnestly, "we'll both work a lot harder tomorrow if we satisfy our appetite for adventure right off."

"Right," Beverly agreed at once. She shook his hand to seal the conspiracy.

"And then we'll have dinner tonight, as promised," he reminded her. "And tomorrow we'll get an early start. Knowing the two of us, we'll have everything tied up in time for a dip in the hotel pool."

"Not me," Beverly said. "As long as there's an ocean around, I won't go near a pool."

"Wait until you see the pool," he said. "And wait until you see the size they grow the waves in this part of the Pacific."

"I can hardly wait." She looked out the window. The plane was circling the airport, and in the distance she could see the crests of waves breaking on smooth white beaches. Further along the shore steep mountains rose, and beyond that were green, mossy hills. "Like a postcard," Beverly whispered, just as the plane released the landing gear. In a moment it had landed on the runway. Another fearless flight, Beverly thought. Her knees weren't even shaking as she walked down the stairs of the plane to the airstrip.

Just inside the lobby Beverly was embraced by a group of women dressed in muumuus, their arms full of flowers. A middle-aged native woman greeted Beverly with a generous smile and slid a string of orchids around her neck. "A lei," Beverly exclaimed, identifying the wreath of flowers the woman had given her. As Beverly thanked the woman and moved toward the door, a second and a third lei were added to the sweetly scented necklace she already wore. "Is this usual?" Beverly asked Sheldon, who was also wearing several wreaths of flowers.

He laughed heartily, his face half covered with orchids. "From my experience, they usually give each passenger one. Once I was given two," he recalled. "But I'm sure it's a mistake. I think they like your red hair."

"I thought it was because I was with you!" she said, lifting a string of flowers to inhale the delicious fragrance.

Their luggage was waiting for them when they reached the hotel. Beverly was willing to admit it was grander than anything in London. They rode the twenty-six flights to the top floor of the modern high rise in a glass elevator that presented a view of the west side of the city. The higher they climbed, the more spectacular the view was.

Beverly could hardly wait to change out of her traveling clothes and explore the island. Once she reached her room, however, she was less hasty to leave. She dropped her purse and briefcase onto the king-size bed and hurried to the window. Sliding glass doors opened onto a spacious balcony. As far as she could see there were miles upon miles of beach. "Oh, Sheldon!" she exclaimed joyfully. "I was wrong to judge Honolulu harshly. This is grand!"

"Pretty impressive," he agreed, casting an approving eye around the room. It was a large room, divided into a sitting room and bedroom by an Oriental screen. "Now change into beachwear. I'll do the same. We'll meet here in thirty minutes."

"That's fine," she said happily. "By the way, where is your room? Are you on this floor?"

"Closer than you might imagine," he said, pointing to a door Beverly hadn't noticed before. "Adjoining rooms." Her smiled faded, but Sheldon kept on grinning. "Locked, of course," he appended. "On both sides. Feel safer?" Beverly nodded shyly. "You didn't think I would go back on my word of honor, did you? After you've proven yourself more indispensable than ever?"

She shook her head, sorry she had doubted him at all. "I'll be ready in no time," she said, resuming her cheerful disposition.

"Good. I'll use this door," he said, opening the door to the hallway. "And we'll keep this one locked, just in case you still have doubts."

Beverly swallowed her embarrassment. "There's no need for that. I don't have any reason to doubt your word," she said, a bit more formally than she intended. But it was probably a good thing to set everything straight from the start. That way they could both relax and have a good, carefree time.

"See you in thirty," he said, closing the door behind him.

Beverly removed her clothes from her suitcase quickly, choosing a bright green shift, from among the new outfits she had bought in London. A quick shower refreshed her, removing the traces of weariness that her excitement hadn't displaced. She dusted herself all over with a film of powder to keep her skin dry in the island's humidity, then slipped into a one-piece swimsuit that clung to the soft curves of her body. Over that she slipped the lightweight shift.

Instead of letting her hair fall around her shoulders, she chose to wear it in double plaits. It made her look younger than her twenty-five years, but she wanted to have the hair off her neck, and her usual style seemed too severe. She completed her outfit with a pair of sandals, leaving her smooth legs bare.

As she filled her duffel bag with lotion, sunglasses, and

the book she was anxious to finish she wondered if she should bring any work along, but she decided against it, choosing to keep the day entirely free. When Sheldon knocked at her door, she was ready to go.

He, too, had changed. He wore a short-sleeved lemon shirt that emphasized his dark skin and a pair of white trousers. His dark hair was wet and combed back neatly from his forehead. He looked as if he had undergone a complete rest cure in the minutes they had been separated. All the concern and responsibility that showed on his face in London had disappeared. Beverly couldn't help noticing how relaxation enhanced his attractiveness.

He pointed out the sights as they rode downstairs in the outdoor elevator. When they reached the front desk, the clerk told him their car was waiting for them outside. Beverly was impressed by the baby-blue Mercedes-Benz convertible he had chosen to rent. "Like it?" Sheldon asked casually.

"Exactly what I would have chosen," she told him, assuming an air of sophistication before giving herself away. "That is, if I had known what to call this kind of car," she said with a laugh.

They left the city directly. Beverly asked the names of the curious sights as they passed them, and by the time they had reached the outskirts of the city she knew a little of the enchanting history of the island.

The roads narrowed. They passed fields of sugarcane like the ones they would use in their advertising. Beverly hastened to note their location, but Sheldon stopped her. "Not today," he admonished. "Work is forbidden today. Even thinking—except of the sun and how good it feels— is taboo. Do you want to offend the gods of hedonism?"

"Who are they?" Beverly asked, not sure he was teasing.

"The fellows who live in the volcanoes, who insist we have a good time and nothing else," he told her. Beverly agreed to forget work. Her braids lifted in the wind as the car raced down the open roads. They passed through a light rain shower, but it served to cool the air; the large, warm drops dried as quickly as they had fallen, and Beverly wondered if Jancie would believe her when she reported this strange weather.

Before long Sheldon turned the car off the road, taking it down an overgrown path. "You seem to know where we're going," Beverly observed. The road was no more than an old cow path, and an abandoned one at that. In front of them she saw that the road abruptly ended.

"I'm letting you in on a secret," he told her. "A friend of mine showed me this spot years ago." He stopped the car at the edge of the cliff, but Beverly couldn't see what lay below. "Until now," Sheldon continued, "I've kept the secret to myself. You'll see why in a minute. But first, you have to promise you'll never bring anyone here, unless they are very deserving." He took the keys from the ignition and placed them in his pocket. "Can I trust you?"

"I'm honored," she said. "And you have my word." Not that she had anyone to tell, she thought.

"Then come with me, Miss Milford." He lifted her bag along with his from the car and shouldered them both. Beverly scurried around the front of the car to join him, excited by the prospect of what lay below. But never in a hundred years was she prepared for the pure and simple beauty, the exhilarating view before her. Down a steep path a cove of virgin-white sand glistened in the sun, surrounded by steep, black rock walls; the ocean was dazzling, so blue it looked almost black; the sun danced on the waves like diamonds around the neck of a dark-skinned native. A line of palm trees bordered the cove. "And it's all for you," Sheldon told her, stepping to one side so that no human figure would obstruct the unspoiled scenery.

"It's almost too much," she whispered breathlessly. "And

no one is here. I would expect the beach to be crowded, it's so perfect. Even the waves are my size."

"No one knows about this place," Sheldon reiterated. "It's a carefully guarded secret. I've never seen anyone here except the friend who brought me the first time, and now you. Now watch your step. The rocks are sharp and loose in places. Here, give me your hand."

She accepted his hand and followed him down the treacherous trail to the beach. They selected a place to spread the blanket Sheldon had secured from the hotel and laid their belongings in the corners. Beverly kicked off her sandals and dug her toes into the warm sand. Her first thought was to strip off her clothes. Without worrying about modesty she pulled her shift over her head and revealed herself clad only in the simple, backless black swimsuit.

Sheldon nodded appreciatively as he unbuttoned his own shirt. Beverly returned his smile, then left him at the blanket and ran to the water. Testing it with her toe, she found it as warm as bathwater; she plunged into a wave and came up the far side of the swell. She turned back to the shore and waved at Sheldon, who was heading for the water.

He didn't pause to test the water but dove straight through the wave. Beverly felt a tug at her leg and panicked before realizing it was Sheldon. He emerged from the water, smiling wickedly, shaking his wet hair onto Beverly. She splashed him with the back of her hand, and he returned the gesture before swimming away from her, leaving Beverly with a mouthful of water. She swam after him, and when he stopped abruptly, she stumbled over him.

They spent the hour frolicking in the waves like baby sea lions. When they finally emerged they were worn out, and the sun-soaked blanket welcomed them like a mother with open arms. Beverly collapsed onto the blanket, her braids dripping. She looked a mess, she knew, but she didn't care.

Sheldon fell down beside her with a moan, and they lay

side by side, too tired to move. She let out a deep breath of satisfaction, her pulse gradually slowing. Her eyes smarted from the salt water; she closed them to block out the sun. "Be careful not to fall asleep in the sun on your first day," he warned gently. "Not with your pale skin. Did you bring any lotion?" Beverly, too tired to move, gestured toward her bag. "I should have known you wouldn't have forgotten anything," he said. "Shall I rub some on your shoulders? You already have some color."

"If you don't mind," Beverly said shyly. She knew the trip would be spoiled if she was uncomfortable with sunburn. She heard him rummaging through the bag until he located the tube of sunscreen, and then she felt his warm hands, cool with lotion, moving expertly over her slender shoulders.

He squeezed more lotion onto his hands and moved them down her back. "Shall I cover your legs too?" he asked.

Beverly swallowed inaudibly. His hands felt so good on her skin, and she hated to stop him. She remembered Sheldon's promise, but she wondered how strong his resolve could be, or hers. "Sure," she said at last, hoping she sounded less nervous than she felt.

He removed his hands from her back to apply more lotion. How thoughtful of him, she thought; he had warmed the chill lotion in his hands before applying it to her warm skin. He touched her calves first, rubbing the lotion into her muscles before moving up her thigh. He avoided the inside of her thigh, as if he knew it would worry her. "What about your arms?" he asked when her legs were covered.

Beverly nodded in appreciation. "It feels so good to lie here indulged," she said.

Sheldon chuckled, but Beverly didn't lift her head to ask why. She felt too good not moving.

After he finished covering her arms he replaced the cap. "Aren't you using some?" she asked.

"I don't really need any," he said. "My skin doesn't burn in the sun."

"How do you stay so tan living in London?" she asked. "I know it's not from lying on the beaches in Brighton."

"Simple, really, My mother was Italian," he told her. "I inherited her dark skin. A couple of hours in the sun, and I retain the color for months."

"Lucky you. A couple of hours in the sun, and I look like a lobster!"

"Then we'll have to take extra special care to see you don't burn while you're here," he said, and Beverly felt her heart churn at his concern.

They lay on the blanket, each quiet with his own thoughts. Beverly assumed he had fallen asleep, but he interrupted the silence after a while to offer her lunch. "Now you are the one who thinks of everything!" she said. "I would have had us starving out here."

"The gods of hedonism would have punished you," he said, pulling a basket of food from his knapsack. There was a plastic container full of shrimp and lobster pieces, a loaf of bread, a pineapple sliced in fourths. He produced a bottle of white wine from a container of ice and a corkscrew; then two pewter wineglasses that caught the sunlight. "To your fair self," he toasted, when the food and wine were arranged in front of them.

Beverly didn't know what to say in response. She should have toasted his thoughtfulness in bringing her to this wonderful place, in thinking to bring their lunch, but instead she simply lifted the glass of wine to her lips and looked up at him over the rim. He held her look boldly before raising his glass and drinking the sweet, cool wine.

Beverly put the stem of her glass into the sand and began to eat. She could hardly stop to wonder if she was eating too fast, the food tasted so good; for some reason she was starving.

After lunch, Beverly rinsed her hands in the ocean, then returned to the towel. She wanted to swim again, but Sheldon warned her to wait until her meal was digested. She folded her hands behind her head and lazily arched her back before settling into the hollow she had carved in the sand. "I sure can't complain about anything at all," she said dreamily, her eyes closed to the bright sun.

"I would have to agree," he said heartily. "But you will if we stay here too much longer." He touched her shoulder with his finger, and when he removed it her skin showed white before returning red. "And," he said, laughing, "when you start complaining I'll be the one who'll have to listen."

She looked over at him. His hair had dried and was falling into his laughing eyes. He was so close to her that Beverly couldn't find a comfortable position to lie in. No matter how she stretched out on the blanket she could feel his presence. Suddenly, hoping to dislodge the thoughts his looks were giving her, she jumped to her feet, careful not to bring sand onto the towel. She scanned the beach, as if expecting to find someone who would rescue her.

"Are you going somewhere?" Sheldon asked. He lay easily on his side, his elbow bent to support his head.

"I thought I'd look for shells," she offered hastily.

"Do you mind if I come along?" he asked, getting to his feet.

"No, not if you want to," she said uneasily. His eyes were still on her.

"Do you have anything to collect them in?" he asked, running his eyes over her damp swimsuit. "I don't see any pockets. Unless you have hidden ones."

Beverly ignored his comment. "I'll bring this basket. It will be perfect for shells." She fought to keep her voice light, but the truth was, whenever she felt uncertain herself, his words, no matter how innocuous, seemed dangerous to her.

They walked across the hot sand until they reached the waterline. The sand was cooler along the shore and hard-packed, so it was less effort to walk.

Sheldon picked up shells as he found them, offering them to Beverly. The half-broken ones he tossed expertly into the sea; they bounced far out over the water, skimming a half-dozen waves. Beverly filled the basket with exquisite shells. Sheldon found a coral-colored ridge with his toe, and when he uncovered it, the shell was larger than both his hands. He offered it proudly to Beverly, and she put it to her ear. A smile formed on her lips when she heard the faint hum of the ocean.

"Let's head back," Sheldon suggested. Beverly's shoulders were red, and her nose was freckling. "You'll have plenty of chances to collect shells while we're filming the commercials."

"Oh?" Beverly exclaimed, surprised. "I thought I would be busy every minute once production began." They had turned back, and Beverly was walking nearest the ocean. A huge wave crashed near the shore, and Sheldon pulled her out of harm's way. His hands on her arms quickened her heartbeat.

"You'll be busy from time to time," he said. "But most of filming is waiting. The actors are really getting paid to appear fresh even though they have to go over the same line fifty times."

"Aren't you exaggerating just a little? Fifty times?"

"I once saw a one-minute commercial take four weeks to film," Sheldon answered. "And it wasn't a particularly difficult assignment."

"Why does it take so long?" Beverly asked, adding one last shell to her collection. They had found a variety of pretty shells, but none matched the coral-colored cone Sheldon had discovered. "I thought we were employing the best actors and staff. Doesn't that insure efficiency?"

"To a degree," Sheldon said, taking her arm again and directing her up the sand toward the blanket. "But it is their expertise that makes things move so slowly. They're perfectionists. Every detail has to be just right, or they insist it be shot over again. And what looks good to the director may not sound right to the sound technician. When the actor has delivered his lines perfectly, the wave hasn't crashed at the right instant, or the sun is at the wrong angle."

"I hadn't realized it was so complex," Beverly admitted, taking one end of the blanket and shaking free the sand. Together they folded it lengthwise, then in half, until they were standing close, their hands touching. "What happens if no one is ever satisfied? Couldn't the filming go on forever?"

"That's where I come in," he said, taking the blanket from her and returning it to the canvas knapsack. "I keep my eye on the budget. A day overtime can cost several thousand pounds. That's why the work we do beforehand is so important. We must never hold up production because of a neglected detail."

"Nothing like applying a little pressure," she charged offhandedly, but she was worried. Would she be up to the job? As much as she had learned during her years with Whitney-Forbes, this was her first time on location. She was now as doubtful as she was inexperienced.

As if reading her mind, Sheldon advised her not to worry. "I brought you along because I knew you would be on top of the job. You always remember what I forget. We're a good team."

"I hope I won't ever disappoint you," she said nervously.

"I'm sure you won't. Here, give me that bundle," he insisted, hoisting the heavy pack onto his shoulders and starting up the trail. Beverly followed, her thoughts already on the list of details she would double-check that night. She was glad she had tomorrow, before the crew arrived, to anticipate any problems. As she reached the top of the path, she thought she would be all right as long as nothing unexpected came up to break her concentration.

She brushed her sandy feet clean before stepping into the car. Sheldon loaded their belongings into the trunk. She checked the mirror and discovered her face was much redder than she had thought. Dozens of tiny freckles had popped out over the bridge of her nose. She brushed the bits of sand from her forehead and looked at her unraveling braids. She was glad it was early enough to allow her plenty of time to repair herself before dinner.

At the hotel Sheldon checked at the front desk for messages.

"Did anyone call while we were out?" she asked in the elevator.

"I have a message to phone Father," Sheldon said uneasily. "I hope nothing has come up. I'll call him upstairs. Say"—he brightened—"what kind of food would you like for dinner?"

"Something authentic?" Beverly suggested. Her eyes widened. "Do you think we could find a luau?"

"We can certainly try," he said amiably. "I'll ask the management. What do you want to do now?" he asked when they reached their floor. "We have a couple of hours before it's even decent to think about eating."

"I'd most like to wash this sand out of my hair," she answered, holding up a wet plait between her thumb and forefinger. "And I should probably finish unpacking."

"Good. I have some things to take care of, too. What do you say we plan for seven thirty. That gives us two hours. Is that enough?"

Beverly dropped her braid and laughed. "If I can't restore myself in that length of time, I don't deserve to eat."

"Fine," he said as they reached her door. "But don't

wash away that glint in your eye, all right? I think this climate becomes you." He was standing very close to her, looking down at her approvingly. Beverly smiled at his compliment. She picked up the conch shell from the basket and offered it to him. He put it next to his ear and listened intently for a minute. "There is a secret in each crash of the wave you hear in this shell," he said seriously. "What do you hear?" he asked, placing the beautiful shell next to her ear.

She heard the gentle roar of the sea, and a far-off hum she couldn't identify, like a call. "The sea," she said. "And something else." She pursed her lips. "Whatever the secret is, I won't tell if you won't." She looked up at him as she handed the shell back to him.

"No," he said. "This is for you to keep. When you find out the secret for sure, let me know." She accepted the shell, but she kept it separate from the others. He looked directly into her eyes, and she felt as if they shared a secret already. It had been such a perfect day. Without a word, he pressed his fingertip to his lip and touched it to her nose. "Sunburn," he said. "Lovely," he added, more to himself than to her. As he walked down the hall to his room, he was whistling an unfamiliar tune.

chapter 10

BEVERLY COULD HEAR the sound of running water from Sheldon's room as she finished rinsing the shampoo from her hair. Her skin felt tight from the day in the sun, and the sharp spray of water made her sunburn hard to ignore. She applied a thin layer of lotion to her body before putting on a light robe.

She felt so refreshed there was no need for a nap. Instead, she opened the doors to the terrace just as the sun started to set over the ocean. Removing the towel from her hair so that the last rays of sunlight could dry it, she settled into a white wicker chair. She threw back her hair and concentrated on the view, wishing she had thought to bring her camera. Jancie would never forgive her for keeping this view to herself.

"Wouldn't a glass of wine make the view all that much prettier?" a familiar voice asked, and Beverly jumped out of her seat. Sheldon stood on the other side of the partition. His hair was wet, and Beverly could see that his skin had darkened two shades. He wore a white cotton shirt opened at the neck, the sleeves rolled back to expose tanned arms, and white shorts that contrasted with his dark legs. The sun glistened on his hair, making him more handsome than ever.

Beverly tore her eyes from him and gestured at the view. "I'm not sure anything would improve this sunset," she said, sighing. "I've never seen anything so spectacular."

"Have a glass of wine, anyway," he urged, pouring a generous amount of sparkling white wine into a goblet. "I have some disappointing news, I'm afraid," he added.

"Disappointing news?" she asked accepting the glass of wine. "Have I forgotten to attend to something?"

"Hardly," he assured her, erasing the frown from her face. "But I'm afraid there isn't a luau on all of Oahu tonight. The management assures me we can have our pick of feasts this weekend. Can you wait? I hear there is a highly reputed Polynesian restaurant just a few minutes' walk from here. Shall we try it?"

"Whatever you think best," she said, happy to place herself in his expert care. "I'm sure any place will be fine." She sipped her wine delicately, looking again at the sky. The blue was streaked with a dozen shades of red. The mountains in the distance were losing detail, turning black as the sun sank behind them. "Are all the sunsets this magnificent?" she asked blissfully.

"Yes," he said simply. "The only thing that bypasses them are the sunrises," he told her. "Which I'm afraid we'll see lots of with our agenda."

"That suits me just fine."

"Not me," he groaned. "I'd be happy if I never saw morning."

"You and Jancie—my roommate," she said. "Well, if I don't see you at breakfast, I'll hammer on your door."

"I'm counting on you. But in fact when it's business I rarely oversleep."

"I thought not," she said playfully. "Just pretend the sun rises at noon here. Would that help?"

He threw his head back in laughter. "Now that's one I haven't yet tried!"

"Oh, did you reach your father?" Beverly asked suddenly, remembering the phone message.

"Not yet," Sheldon said seriously. "I've tried twice, but without luck."

"I hope nothing is the matter."

"I'm sure it's nothing. Probably just wanted to hear that we arrived safely." But Beverly was doubtful, and Sheldon looked more concerned than he sounded. Douglas Whitney was hardly accustomed to confirming his son's flight arrivals. "Could you be ready for dinner before seven thirty?" Sheldon asked impulsively.

"I think so," she said. She touched her hand to her hair and found it was dry. "I just need to dress. I only need a few minutes."

"That's what I like," he said. "Spontaneity." His face was bright with approval.

"What do you have in mind?" she asked gaily.

"I thought a walk in the last minutes of daylight would be nicer than standing on opposite sides of this partition."

She looked at the setting sun doubtfully. "I'm not sure I can be ready that quickly. But it looks like there's a nearly full moon coming up. And I'd love to walk." After all the relaxing they had done that day, she thought exercise might release some of the energy she had stored.

"Great. We'll take a look at the city and eat when we get hungry."

"Sounds great!" she said before returning indoors.

Quickly she brushed her hair, delighted to find gold highlights in it from the day in the sun. It felt like silk beneath her hand, and she pinned the waves of hair behind one ear with a pink hibiscus.

She slid effortlessly into the strapless pink crepe de chine dress that André had given her and zipped it up. A thin veil of voile covered the skirt of the dress, but the bodice was cut simply across her bosom. Her bare shoulders had freckled, and she had to admit she liked the effect the sun had had on her coloring. Slipping her feet into delicate sandals, she stood back from the mirror and was approving the results when Sheldon knocked on the door.

"I'm ready," she called as he opened the door.

"I see!" he said appreciatively. "That effort would have taken some girls I know several hours, with not nearly so pleasing results." His remark had been meant as a compliment but it jolted Beverly, and her smile faded. He cleared his throat to cover his mistake. "You look very pretty, Beverly."

She smiled again tentatively. He had exchanged his white shirt and shorts for a dark blue jacket and trousers and a shirt a lighter shade of blue. He had taken a baby orchid from the lei and placed it in his buttonhole. He looked stunning. "You look good, too," she told him shyly.

She took his arm, and they left the hotel for their evening walk. The sun had disappeared, but a three-quarter moon rose in the dark sky to light their way. They strolled for an hour, looking in store windows, watching the people on the streets, talking aimlessly until Sheldon suggested dinner. Beverly agreed readily.

It took three waiters to bring the food to their table, and a fourth brought cooking utensils and masterfully sliced, cooked, and served the entree before them, a healthy portion of vegetables and beef dressed in a heavenly golden sauce. When Beverly had tasted the first bite and expressed her delight, the chef disappeared to another table, leaving them alone to enjoy their meal.

"This is delicious," Beverly commented again. "The sauce is both spicy and sweet. I wonder how they do it?"

"I don't know," Sheldon admitted. "But it is superb."

They ate their meal eagerly, talking little. The out-of-doors had increased both their appetites. It wasn't until dessert that Sheldon brought up the next day's activities.

"We have a choice for tomorrow," he began, popping a juicy wedge of pineapple into his mouth. "We have to take a look at the location spot that was recommended to us. We could do that first thing in the morning or wait until afternoon. I suggest we spend the morning making phone calls and the like. I'll take care of renting a plane for us."

Beverly choked on her dessert. "A plane?" she asked. "But I thought we were going to go by boat and . . . and *stay* there!" Misery was clouding her eyes. "Are we going to fly back and forth every day?"

"I don't think we'll find accommodations suitable to our needs. It's primitive, at least where we will be. Just a few shacks. Unspoiled country. Perfect for our filming." Beverly didn't say anything. She couldn't. Sheldon settled back, sipping his coffee. "If it hadn't been for you, Bev, we would have hired a London model to promote the packaged product. You're responsible for this stroke of genius."

Beverly promised herself to keep quiet next time she had a "good" idea. Just when she thought she had cured her phobia of flying she was faced with the demon itself again, flying in a small plane over treacherous waters to uninhabited territory. Would she ever survive, even if the plane did? She would be a bundle of nerves, entirely useless to the production. She *had* to find a way of staying there once they arrived. She thought she could manage the first flight, but she would never be able to climb aboard the tiny plane twice a day.

"I'm looking forward to the trip," Sheldon told her. "It's been years since I last flew, and this is exactly the kind of flying I enjoy most."

"You're planning to fly the plane yourself?" she asked in shock.

He looked hurt. "Now don't sound so mistrustful," he said. "I'm a damn good pilot, if I do say so myself. I've been flying since I was a kid."

He looked to Beverly for some kind of response, but she couldn't say anything. She just looked down at her unfinished dessert, her appetite gone. She thought she would be ill if she sat there a minute longer. "Can we go?" she asked.

"Certainly," he said, watching her closely. "Are you all right?" he asked. "You've gone entirely white."

"I'll be all right once we're outside," she said, hoping it was true.

"Let's go," he said, helping her to her feet and leading her to the door. Beverly waited in front of the restaurant, trying to catch her breath, while Sheldon saw to the bill. She was grateful for his steady arm as they walked back to the hotel.

Sheldon continued to watch her, not comprehending the abrupt change in her behavior, and his puzzled consternation only increased her anxiety.

Inside the hotel she asked to be excused, but Sheldon insisted he accompany her to her room. They stepped into the elevator, but now the view of the city from the glass cage made Beverly think of the tiny plane she was expected to ride in every day for the next week. She kept her eyes on the numbers above the door, avoiding the view altogether, avoiding Sheldon's concerned, questioning eyes.

At her door, she tried once again to extricate herself from his concern. "I'm sorry, Sheldon," she said weakly. "I just need to lie down."

"Should I phone the hotel doctor? You look so pale."

"Please, no," she said. "I just need to rest."

"If you're sure," he agreed doubtfully. "I'll be right next door. Will you call me—or just knock on the wall—if there is *anything* I can do to help?"

She tried to express her thanks, but his solicitude increased her dizziness. "Yes," she promised, raising her eyes to his. He looked down at her, his dark eyes deeply troubled. He touched his hand to her forehead. It was damp and feverish.

"Promise you'll call me?"

"Yes," she agreed again. Reluctantly he left her alone.

Quickly she stripped off her dress and left it at the foot of her bed, not having the energy to hang it up or put on a nightgown. She lay in bed naked. Her whole body burned with fever, as if she had suddenly contracted a rare flu, but Beverly knew the truth was that the depths of her fear were being realized. She had suppressed her fear to endure the long flight from London. Now that she had to call upon an even greater store of courage, the buried fear insisted on asserting itself.

She lay for a long time in the darkened room, not daring to move lest she be sick. She could hear movement from the other room, and she knew Sheldon was waiting to hear if she was in need. Try as she might she could not quiet her nerves, and when she heard him tap on the wall, she tapped back in spite of herself.

In seconds he was at her door, and she had time barely to cover her body with her thin robe before he was in the room. "Are you feeling better?" he asked cautiously, but one look at her informed him she was still shaky. He led her back to bed, insisting she lie down.

He disappeared into the bathroom and returned with a damp washcloth, which he pressed over her forehead. Beverly felt a chill run down her spine, but the cold felt good on her brow. She started to thank him, but he urged her not to speak.

He left her bedside to phone downstairs, for a doctor. She knew she had to tell him the truth. He might fire her for being such a coward, but she couldn't let him continue to seek a remedy for something as incurable as fear. "Sheldon," she whispered softly.

"Shhhh, just lie still," he said gently, touching her arm with his steady hand. "The doctor will be here soon. He's out of the hotel at present, but they're looking for him. They promised they'd call back when they located him."

"But it won't do any good," she admitted unhappily. She sat up in bed, the front of her robe falling open to reveal her naked breast, but she was too concerned with her confession to care about her immodesty. Sheldon didn't seem to notice. He was entirely concerned with her well-being. "I don't need a doctor," she said.

"Do you know what's wrong with you?" he asked. She nodded, ashamed. "Can you tell me?" he implored. His voice was kind, inviting her confidence, but she could hardly speak.

"I—it's nothing . . . physical," she managed, before collapsing into tears. "It's—"

"Take it slowly," he said, trying to make her lie back against the pillows. "Take your time."

Beverly looked at him, her green eyes bright with tears and uncertainty, her lashes black and matted. She tried to speak, but again she was overcome with emotion. She lay back trembling.

Sheldon sat beside her, looking helpless. "Please," he pleaded. "Tell me what I can do for you. You're breaking my heart." He took her small hand in his. She squeezed his hand, trying to convey her thanks, but all she could do was cry. When the phone rang, he answered it at once; it was the front desk. They had found the doctor, but he was an hour away.

Sheldon covered the receiver with his hand as he relayed the information to Beverly. "Shall I have them call someone else?" he asked. Beverly shook her head adamantly, trying to tell him a doctor wouldn't help. He held the phone, contemplating the situation. "I'll tell you what," he said resolutely to Beverly. "I'll tell the desk to forget the doctor if you'll tell me what's the matter."

Beverly nodded her head, and Sheldon returned to the phone. He asked that the doctor check with him first thing in the morning. Then he turned to Beverly and waited. Her tears had subsided somewhat, but she didn't trust herself to speak. "Come, now, you promised you'd explain," he urged her.

"I—I'm—" she started, but once again her voice faltered, and she looked to him to help her. She wished he could read her mind so that she didn't have to talk about her fear. She wished he would take her in his arms and comfort her, but he made no attempt to move, to physically soothe her. He simply held her damp hand and waited for her to speak. "I'm so frightened!" she began, tears brimming over and falling down her face.

How could she explain her fear to Sheldon, a man who didn't fear anything or anyone? Surely he would scorn her, laugh at her. Surely he would never trust her with the kind of responsibility he had begun to delegate to her. He would see her for what she was, a silly coward, never to be treated with respect . . . never to be loved. She tasted the salt of her tears and tried to free her hand from his to wipe them from her face. "I'm a coward!" she said at last, her words nearly drowned by tears.

But now that she had started, he might as well know the whole truth. If he was going to be rid of her, it might as well be before her fear ruined the trip any further. "I'm terrified of flying," she continued slowly. "My husband died in a plane crash, flying over the ocean in one of those small planes. He was a pilot," she explained. "And he had no fear of anything, like you. We had been married only a month when his plane crashed. I vowed never to fly again—I never wanted to—but when you insisted that I accompany you to Paris, well, I was glad to face my fears. I thought . . ." Her voice faltered again, but Sheldon implored her to finish. "I thought I had overcome my fear!" she explained. "I knew I would never enjoy flying, but at least I wasn't sick to my stomach, as I had been flying to London the first time from New York. But now," she said, a sob breaking through, "now, I don't think I can stand to fly in one of those little planes every day, back and forth from Hawaii. I'm so afraid—I won't be able to think of anything but the next flight. I won't be able to do my job. And I so wanted to make you proud of me. I wanted to do a great job for you."

Sheldon had been listening intently, a sadness darkening his eyes. "Why didn't you tell me this before?" he asked. "I would have never insisted you travel with me if I had known of your fear."

"I thought you knew," she declared. "I thought you knew the reason I transferred jobs from New York was because of my husband's death."

"I guess I did know something about it. Father told me you had suffered a personal loss, but he didn't tell me more, and I didn't think it right to pry. Honestly, Beverly, I wouldn't have thought to bring you along had I known. I'm so sorry."

"Do you hate me?" she asked ashamedly. She had to know if he was going to send her home shamefaced, or demote her, or fire her. She didn't know which fate would be worse.

"Hate you?" he asked incredulously. "I was thinking you must hate me, for being so insensitive to your fear. I mean, if you thought I *knew* about your husband's death and your fear, you must have thought me heartless to insist you fly."

"Oh, no," she assured him. "I thought you expected me to rise above my fears. I tried, but I just can't do it," she said, new tears running down her face. "Are you going to send me back?"

"Oh, Beverly," he said tenderly, his gaze settling on her trembling lip. He bent toward her and slowly brought her face to his. He kissed away the tears from her mouth, then her eyes, covering her dampened face with his lips, coaxing her, seducing her gently out of her fear, her sadness.

"I can stay?" she managed to ask, her chin quivering as she tried to hold back the tears. He took her in his arms, and she wrapped her own arms around his strong neck, clinging to him, holding him tightly. He held her ardently, but his words were soft, reassuring.

He kissed the side of her face, her hair, her mouth again. She swallowed a distressed sob as he took her sadness from her. He pressed her to him dearly as his lips parted hers. She received his kiss, her passion mounting as his tongue explored the inside of her lower lip. She clung to him newly, but it was no longer out of sorrow. She continued to shake, but now it was with longing. The more he kissed her, the more she wanted him, but she couldn't find the words to tell him. She buried her head in his chest as she felt his mouth moving from her ear to her neck, his lips brushing away her tumbled hair, and down to the opening of her robe, until his hungry mouth reached her breasts. His hands followed his lips, separating her robe, before he pulled himself from her to see what he had revealed. "God, you are beautiful, Beverly," he said in hushed appreciation. He looked into her moist eyes and silently asked permission to break the vow that had kept him from her.

She met his gaze with unmasked desire and answered him by bringing his mouth back to hers, bruising his lips with her fevered kisses. "Hold me," she cried. Her body quivered uncontrollably. She arched her back to be closer to him, and he held the small of her back with one hand

and cupped her breast with the other.

She closed her eyes as his hand moved down her stomach, as light as a feather, calling up an excitement she had never known. Just as she thought she would cry out in ecstasy, he suspended his lovemaking. He leaned over her and lifted her from the bed, disentangling her robe from her body and leaving her naked. He held her in one arm, her arms wrapped securely around his neck, as he pulled back the covers on the bed and placed her in the middle. She shuddered in expectation. She looked up at him, waiting for him to join her, but he covered her and tucked the blankets around her. She waited breathlessly as he turned out the light, her heart pounding loudly beneath the soft folds of the satin sheets. "Sheldon?" she asked in the darkness.

His voice reached her from across the room. "Yes, dear," he answered gently.

"Are you leaving?" she asked in horror. Her voice choked with humiliation as she understood that he was not planning to stay with her.

"I can't stay, Bev," he said quietly, his voice apologetic. "I promised I wouldn't make love to you, and I just came close to breaking a promise I intend to keep."

"But I want you to stay," she said, abandoning her pride. "I need you to stay with me."

He returned to her bed and sat beside her. She could see his face in the faint moonlight, and he looked as miserable as she felt. She didn't understand what had happened. He seemed to enjoy her kisses as much as she had his. Could it be that the sight of her body unclothed had repulsed him? Had robbed him of his appetite? She had to know. "Why won't you stay?"

"If I stay, Bev, you'll hate me in the morning. I would be taking advantage of your sorrow, or you would think I had. You almost quit a job you love because I tried to force myself on you." She tried to protest, but he stopped her.

"I don't mean to put work before our relationship—you must know you are more important than the job—but if you wake up disillusioned and quit the job, the commercial tomorrow will be impossible. How would I explain the lost contract to Father?"

Beverly tensed with indignation. So that was it. Work first. Just as always. He didn't care about her. He was willing to have her, but not if it risked losing the contract. "I see," she said coolly, all the emotion erased from her voice.

"No, I don't think you do," he countered. "I want you, Beverly, more than I want anything. But I don't want you upset. I don't want you to think I was acting concerned to trick you into bed. You were really upset a while ago. You didn't trust me enough to tell me your fear."

"Because I didn't want you to think me a coward," she repeated.

"Do you really want to make love to a man you thought would chastise you? You aren't an unreasonable woman. That must make me an unreasonable man. When I come to your bed, I want you to trust me implicitly." He shook his head slowly. "All you needed to do was tell me," he said. "I wouldn't have insisted you come to Hawaii or to Paris with me," he said. "Though I'm thankful beyond words that you did come, both times."

"You aren't angry?" she asked.

"What kind of person do you think I am?" he asked incredulously. "Some kind of monster who cares nothing for your fears?"

"But you don't seem to fear anything," she said. "And I *don't* know who you are, Sheldon. Sometimes you're so kind to me, and sometimes you act like you'd like to murder me."

A smile curled his lips. "That's because both are true. Sometimes I wish you had never entered my life, and sometimes I forget my name in your presence."

"But why? What do I do?" she asked, not understanding.

"You little fool. Why do you think?" He stared at her, a frustrated look on his face. She shrugged her shoulders; she really didn't know what to think. "Because I'm mad for you," he said desperately. "And because you so clearly don't trust me I can't bring myself to make love to you, when I know my actions will strengthen your mistrust. That quite possibly you'll quit the job in the morning. And I would rather be near you like this, as ridiculous as that may seem, than have you fully for one night and lose you in the morning. Now do you understand? Do you understand why I'm going back to my room in spite of thh fact that every muscle in my body is straining to lie with you?"

His voice had risen to a crescendo. He was pacing the room, gesturing frantically. Beverly couldn't believe her ears. She stared at him blankly. Could he be telling the truth? Her head swelled in confusion. "Are you saying that you love me—really love me, Sheldon?" she asked in disbelief.

"Purely and simply," he told her seriously.

"And that's why you won't sleep with me?" she asked, still not comprehending.

"Exactly. Do you think if I didn't care about you so much I would think twice about making love to you? Why do you think I stopped just now, when I'm burning for you all over?"

"I thought you couldn't stand the sight of me," she confessed timidly. "I thought you took one look and lost interest."

Sheldon groaned heavily. "You are a fool. Don't you know that I've had to tie my hands to my sides ever since you started working for me. You drive me crazy with desire! And if that wasn't bad enough, I had to fall in love with you. And you never gave me a second thought, except to mistrust me and to question my motives. That's why I can't take advantage of your unhappiness. I know you would return to London, to your boyfriend, and hate me more than ever while my own love had increased. I don't think I could stand that, not after I had possessed you completely and wanted you again."

Beverly stared at him blankly. Nothing made sense. Sheldon Whitney, the man who could, and did, have any woman he wanted, was telling her he feared her rejection? Impossible! "But why did you make love to Lizzie Sexton, and all the others, if you wanted to love me?" she asked, giving him the opportunity to confess that this was all a joke.

"Because you made it clear you wanted nothing to do with me. And I had to do something to dissipate my sexual frustration. Those women didn't matter to me. Don't you see? No one has mattered to me since you moved to London." He stopped pacing to look at her. "Why couldn't you have loved me?" he asked, looking down at the floor in misery.

"But I do!" she said quickly. He looked up at her abruptly, as if daring her to continue her lie. "I didn't know it at first," she explained. "And I did resent your promiscuity, but I couldn't help but love you, even though I tried to fight it, in the same way I can't fight my fear of planes."

He stared at her. "What about your boyfriend? Aren't you telling him the same thing you're asking me to believe now?"

"I have to confess," she said, "that I haven't a clue who you think I date. I see no one!"

"Who gives you flowers twice a week?" he demanded harshly.

Beverly blinked. "Is that who you think I date?" she asked, laughing. Sheldon nodded. "But that's the funniest thing I've ever heard! If you could see the dear old man who gives me the flowers! Because he hates to see me so lonely! The Bond Street flowerman gave me those roses."

"Are you telling me the truth?" he asked doubtfully.

"Yes!" she insisted. "I never even knew his name."

Sheldon was beginning to understand that the joke was on him. Laughter began to ripple from deep within him, as much in relief as in humor. Soon it was rolling out of him, and Beverly was forced to join with him.

They both laughed so hard that neither of them could stop. Tears, for the second time that night, glistened in Beverly's eyes. She reached for Sheldon, and he took her in his arms, the laughter subsiding. "I can't believe that I've been jealous of him," Sheldon confessed, visualizing the homely old gent. He looked at her happily, then remembered something else. "Why wouldn't you have dinner with me?"

"You know your reputation as well as I do. I was determined not to be another one of your trophies."

Sheldon cringed. "Reputations always overstate the truth."

"Don't give me that line," she said severely. "Even if one tenth of your reputation is true, that was enough to keep me away. Besides," she added, "I lost the man I loved after one month of marriage. I had vowed never to love again."

"And now?" he asked solemnly.

"And now I've lost all my good sense, all my willpower. I tried not to love you, but I failed. I do love you," she said simply.

"When did you first lose the battle?" he asked, his face lighting with joy at her admission.

"In Paris. In the garden outside André and Celeste's house, I was pretty sure. The next day I knew for certain. I'm surprised you didn't know."

"I thought you were interested in André," he said. "What *did* you do to convince him to sign the contract so agreeably?"

"I certainly didn't sleep with him!" she said indignantly. "Is that what you thought?"

"He is an attractive man, and he was giving *me* so much trouble with the conditions of the contract. He's known to like things his way."

"But he's married!"

"But he signed the contract after a day alone with you."

Beverly had to laugh. "No wonder you were so cold to me. If I had anything to do with the signing, it must have been André's guilt."

"Guilt?" he asked.

"He had to cancel our date," she explained. "I toured the city alone, and he felt very badly." She told him about her journey through the streets of Paris, of the cathedral and the stained-glass windows. "That's when I knew for sure I loved you." She remembered the child in the museum. "I even thought of the beautiful child you and I might have had." Her eyes glistened at the memory. "I sometimes think I would rather have your child than anything else in the world!"

Sheldon released a deep sigh. "Why didn't you tell me?" he asked.

"You were barely talking to me, remember?" He frowned. "And I wasn't going to make any special effort," she had to admit, "once I saw you in the bar with—that woman—"

"Now that wasn't what it looked like!" he insisted. "I left the bar as soon as I saw you. I—I even came to your room. I knocked on your door, but you weren't there, or you weren't answering. By then I was sure you hated me."

"Well, you were the only one," she said. "Celeste and André both knew at once. Even your father knew," she recalled. "Except for me, you were the only one who didn't know," she said teasingly. "Oh, aren't we foolish to let our pride stand in the way? I should have asked you why you were upset. Then I would have known. Next time I will, I promise." She snuggled into his strong arms. "Have I told you too much?" she asked, suddenly doubtful. "Do you still think you love me?"

"No," he said abruptly, and Beverly froze in his arms. "I *know* I love you. Are you sure you love me?"

"Absolutely," she said, hugging him happily.

"Can you guess the secret of the seashell now?" he asked seductively.

She caught the glint in his eye. "Hmmm. I think I'm beginning to understand. Does it have anything to do with your staying the night?"

"It might," he said. "Then again . . . But before I devour you, I have a question. First, are you going to feel the same in the morning as you do now?"

"Probably better," she quipped, and he swatted her playfully.

"Secondly," he went on. "And don't get me wrong. You know you're more important to me than all of Whitney-Forbes. But we're going to have about eighteen people depending on us to survey the location tomorrow. How are you going to feel about waking up at sunrise and flying to Hawaii with me?"

She looked at him anxiously, trying to collect her thoughts before speaking. "First," she started, "I will never feel good about flying in a tiny plane, sunrise or not. But I think I can manage it if you're with me. Telling you about my fear has helped. And I do think it's a good idea for our love to benefit Whitney-Forbes, not bring it to collapse. I don't intend to sleep tonight! I have to find out if your reputation is justified. Jancie calls you the 'King of Passion'!"

"Could it be that I've met my match?" he asked slyly.

"Wouldn't that be nice," she retorted, before pulling back the covers to invite him into her bed.

It took Sheldon just moments to remove his clothes, but by the time he was undressed Beverly's shyness had returned. She watched the strong, bold lines of his powerful body with a mixture of appreciation and nervousness, feeling very small and inexperienced as he moved into bed and enveloped her in his arms. He must have sensed her doubts, because he was slow and gentle with her, starting his lovemaking all over again. The lips that had burned against hers earlier that evening now touched hers delicately. A new kind of shiver started through her body. He was in no hurry. He languished kisses on her mouth, her neck, then drifted into the thick blanket of her hair, as if he was satisfied to spend all his time kissing and holding her, as if to take more was beyond his experience.

Beverly yielded to his kisses, freed now by her certainty of his love for her. As the last doubt disappeared, her passion reasserted itself, and she kissed his mouth with fervor. Her hands strayed downward from the nape of his neck, feeling his hard muscles beneath her fingertips. She wrapped her arms around him so tightly that she feared she would take his breath away, but her embrace only increased his own strength, his own grip around her.

He lifted his face from the sweet hollow of her neck and looked at her beseechingly, covering her again with kisses before moving down from her throat to her breast. He discovered her again with his tongue, and her nipples rose as he flicked her with his tongue, then covered her breast with his warm mouth.

His hand slid down over her small hips onto her thighs and his mouth left her breast to follow his hands. She could feel his breath on her damp skin, and his lips pursued her with the same tenderness with which he had kissed her breasts. The sharp pang of desire spun into madness until Beverly was not sure she could restrain herself. She moved to his touch, her breath becoming short and desperate. As the sensation increased, she let out a deep moan. Without knowing her own strength, she held him until her hands went white. In total abandon, she dug her fingernails into his arms.

The wave of momentum subsided into a gentle swell of passion. Sheldon brought her back into his arms, his cool body tense against her dewy skin. He smoothed the tangled hair back from her brow and kissed her closed eyes so lightly that she thought she had imagined it. She looked at him, and the hunger in his eyes renewed her desire for him. More than anything she wanted to give him the pleasure he had given her.

She bit playfully at his lower lip. She could taste her desire on his lips. She moved downward, tasting the salt of his chest against her mouth. She ran her hand through the dark mass of hair which covered his chest, down to his smooth muscular stomach. His skin was so soft she laid her face against it, before tasting his strength. Sheldon moaned at her touch, and his pleasure heightened her own. Suddenly he pulled her to him and she could feel the direction of his passion.

No longer were his kisses gentle. His lips were hard against her mouth, and he moved with determined strength, searching for her soul with the center of his being. Beverly threw back her head at the aching pleasure he gave her; swayed under his weight; held him as he moved. She felt herself rise to meet him, her impatience equal to his. Together they clung to each movement, like graceful dancers, knowing each other's moves as their own. She felt at one with him. Her soul started to melt into his, and he must have known, for he quickened his pace to meet hers until they dissolved into liquid, filling the room with the song of their love.

Her heartbeat competed with his as he lowered himself beside her. She ran a finger over his damp chest and rested her head on his shoulder. He encircled her waist with one arm, and they lay together peacefully, not yet believing the power of their love.

In spite of her determination to stay awake, Beverly closed her eyes to savor the sweet satisfaction that engulfed her, and before she could stop herself she was asleep. Sheldon must have slept too, but for how long, she didn't know. She woke cradled in his warm arms, as at home in his embrace as if she had spent years lying next to him.

He must have felt her stir, for he opened his eyes, and his look told Beverly that he too felt good in their embrace. She had thought fleetingly that he might wake dismayed to find her beside him—that once his urge had been satisfied, he would rather sleep elsewhere—but his sleepy smile assured her otherwise. He pulled her nearer to him and touched her face with his lips.

They savored the details of each other's faces, as if to memorize every nuance, line, and feature. Suddenly he looked questioningly at her and his face altered, a faint line deepening between his brows. Beverly reached up to soothe away any doubts. He smiled at her touch, and the joy brought light to his eyes. His lips softened when he smiled. It would take her years before she knew his face well, and she hoped each day would give her more time to study him, know him, understand his thoughts before he spoke them.

His dark eyes penetrated her own, and she understood that his desire had returned, just at the moment when she felt hers mounting within her. The warmth that lay between them burst into flames of passion. Sheldon's gentle touch now burned her. They moved to embrace the heat, to build the flames into fire, to consume one another, to be consumed. Their brief sleep had taken their love into their unconsciousness, and now that it was reintroduced to wakefulness nothing could stand in its way. Beverly watched Sheldon rise above her, and she moved to hold him with all of her body. The more she possessed him, the more she wanted him: like oxygen, he fueled her fire. The flames grew higher, surrounding her like waves. Her will was lost to his, and she liquefied under his hard demands, trusting that he would guide her out of this blaze. She closed her eyes as the fire consumed her, shuddered from the heat, until together they extinguished their fever, brought their fused bodies into the cool safety of satisfaction.

Sheldon fell back dramatically, groaning in disbelief. Beverly brought the damp washcloth from the bedside table to his brow. He opened his eyes as she blew cool breath over his dampened forehead, and seeing that she was smiling and happy, he fell asleep, and she soon followed.

They slept and woke throughout the night, and each time Beverly was surprised by the renewal of desire, no matter how many times they exhausted it. At the first hint of daylight, Beverly removed herself from Sheldon's embrace as quietly as she could, but her slight movement woke him. "Where are you going?" he asked fearfully. "Are you leaving?"

She touched her hand to his sleepy body. "I'm not going far," she assured him. "But it's morning, and I thought I would order us breakfast. Sleep a little while longer."

Sheldon rolled over to look out the window. A faint halo of light challenged the night. He could hardly see the color of the sky. "It's not morning yet," he complained. "We have several hours still. Are you really going to insist we get up?"

She smiled at him indulgently. She was wide awake. "No, you sleep. I'll tell them to serve us breakfast in an hour, all right?" He smiled sleepily, and when she returned from the bathroom, he was sleeping deeply.

Quietly she called room service and ordered two meals brought up to the room at seven o'clock. Then she returned to the bathroom, and much as she hated to erase any traces of their lovemaking, she stepped into the shower and scrubbed herself clean. So as not to disturb Sheldon, she used the bathroom mirror to fix her hair and apply a touch of makeup. In spite of the little sleep she had had she looked vibrant, her eyes alive and alert, her cheeks glowing and healthy.

When she reentered the bedroom the day was light enough for her to select her clothes without turning the light on. She removed a skirt and sleeveless cotton blouse from the wardrobe and put them on over her lace brassiere and panties. "You look better without all those clothes on," Sheldon remarked, startling her. She spun around to find him awake, lying on his side, watching her.

"How long have you been watching me?" she demanded. She wasn't used to being observed.

"Not long enough. Come here," he urged, and Beverly returned to sit beside him. His body was still warm and sleepy, and she had to resist a temptation to climb back into bed. He stroked her bare arm with his long middle finger, renewing the chills that had kept her awake most of the night. "Do you know what I would like most in the world?" he said tenderly.

She leaned down to accept a kiss from him. "No, what?" she asked.

"To spend the rest of my life watching you in your private moments. I've never seen you more beautiful than just now, making decisions about your dress, unnoticed, alone in your own world." She laughed at him, but she was touched by his words. "Can I join you in your private world?" he asked poignantly. "Ahhh, if only that were possible."

"But I want to have you share my life," she said. "Why is that impossible?" She tried to conceal the hurt in her voice. Was he trying to let her down gently?

"We can share a lot," he agreed, "but I want to know your every thought before you speak it. I want to see your every movement, without you knowing you're being observed."

"We could get a one-way mirror," she suggested happily. "Would that help?"

"You know why I love you so much?" he asked suddenly.

"Because I let you sleep late in the morning?"

"Hardly." he said. "It's because you always have such crazy ideas. How about coming back to bed?" he implored.

"How about you getting up instead?" she suggested. "Breakfast will be here soon, and it's embarrassing enough that you're dining in my room this early, let alone sleeping in my bed. We'll have to mess the sheets in your room so the maid won't know!" Her eyes twinkled.

"Always seeing to the details, aren't you? But the maid won't care where I slept. Do you mind people knowing?" he asked her. She lowered her eyes to her hands in her lap. "You do!" he said. "Are you ashamed of me?" he asked, hurt.

"I'm not ashamed of you, at all," she told him truthfully. "But I am a little embarrassed. After all—"

"Because we're not married?" he guessed.

"I know it's pretty old-fashioned of me, but it's just the way I've always lived my life. I've never had to think about what it looks like before."

"Well, get used to it," he said stubbornly. "Because I plan to spend a lot of time in your room. Regardless of what the maid thinks." He smiled at her boldly and tried to pull her back to bed, but the knock on the door saved the day. He ducked into the shower as she answered the door.

When he had finished bathing, he slipped through the adjoining door to his room for his clothing, and Beverly had to laugh: the door wasn't locked on both sides; in fact, it hadn't been locked on either side.

She poured coffee for the two of them when Sheldon returned. They devoured the food in front of them, their appetites ravenous from the night of love.

"How do you feel about this little trip today?" he asked, when they had finished eating breakfast.

Beverly took the dishes from the table and set them on trays by the door. "I feel nervous," she admitted. "But I can stand it."

"Maybe we *can* rent a house on Hawaii. That way all you have to think about is today's flight and the one at the end of the week. Would that make you feel better?"

"Oh, Sheldon, could we?" She beamed. "That would solve everything!"

"Why don't you ask the travel agent in the lobby if she knows of any places we can rent? Besides," he added, "we would be away from the rest of the crew, and I would have less chance of losing you."

She looked at him uncomprehendingly. "Losing me? You mean to other men?" Sheldon nodded quickly. "There's little chance of that, no matter where we stay," she insisted. "Remember, you're the flirt, not me."

"Not anymore," he chimed. "You are content with just me?" he asked shyly.

"Sheldon Whitney! That's the silliest question you've ever asked. If I had to choose between you and food, I'd choose you!"

He grinned at her. "I'm glad you don't have to make that choice." He brought her into his arms and lifted her smiling face to his, taking a deep, satisfying kiss before releasing her. "I sure do hate to go to work right now," he confessed, and Beverly nodded in agreement. "But since we must, I am mighty glad you're coming with me."

chapter 11

"DID YOU REACH your father?" Beverly asked as they settled down to work. They had decided to spend the morning making arrangements from the hotel and fly to Hawaii in the early afternoon, once they were sure they wouldn't be needed back on the mainland. The agent downstairs had located a rental she thought suitable on the island of Hawaii. She had warned Beverly it would be simple, but Beverly knew it wouldn't matter as long as she wasn't faced with the commute each day. As long as Sheldon was with her.

They had converted Sheldon's room into their office, and Beverly enjoyed working at the other end of the room from him. Each time she looked up from her work, or as she was getting off the phone, he was there; more often than not he had chosen that moment to look up from his work. Their eyes locked momentarily, conveying their love; then they returned to their work. It was demanding to work with the one she loved.

"I tried again while you were downstairs. I'm starting to worry. They said he's been gone from the office since

Monday morning. No one knows where he went, but he said something to his secretary about not being in all week. Most unusual. I don't think Father has missed a day of work his entire life."

"Like his son?" Beverly teased, trying to relieve his worry.

Sheldon eyed her dangerously. "*I* was willing to skip work today. It was you who insisted I get out of bed."

Beverly feigned innocence. "Who, me?" she tried, but when Sheldon threatened to leave his work, she changed her approach. "There will be plenty of time for play *later*," she reminded him, lifting the key to the house rental and dangling it in front of her.

"You're playing with fire, Miss Milford," he warned her.

"I know," she said. She held his gaze for as long as she could before breaking into laughter. "If I can just think about what I can expect *after* we get there, I'll have a better chance enduring the flight over!"

"Shall I give you something to rekindle your expectations?"

"I don't think there is any need for that. My memory isn't that poor! I can still feel you in every part of me." She sighed deeply. "It's nearly impossible to concentrate on work when I would rather think about you," she said. There would always be that temptation now, to leave their work unfinished and continue their lovemaking. "I think I can finish in another couple of hours," she said. "That is, if I can keep my mind *on* work enough to complete it."

"I'll try to help you," he said, rising. "I have some business here in town. Finish up what you have to do while I'm gone. Don't forget to pack. If this place works out, you won't have to fly back here until the shoot is over."

"Good thinking. When will you be back?" she asked, not wanting him to go at all.

He glanced at his watch. "It's nine o'clock now. Will

you be finished by noon?" Beverly nodded. She was sure she could manage everything, especially with him out of her sight.

He was standing in front of the open terrace doors, the breeze caressing the sleeves of his shirt. Beverly went to his side, and he wrapped his arms around her and kissed her. Even the three hours they would be apart were too many now. She knew she was being silly, but she couldn't help it. Sometimes emotions just wouldn't listen to reason. "Hurry back," she encouraged. "I'll miss you."

He looked at her seriously. "Yes, I'll miss you too. How did we survive until now, without our love for each other?" She shook her head, wondering the same thing. "All I can say is that I'm glad not to have to pretend any longer." Beverly smiled shyly. She wondered how long this bliss could last. What would become of them when they returned to London, to the demands of the office routine? Would his love for her survive the trip home?

As if reading her thoughts, he kissed her again. "I'll never stop loving you," he told her. "We're in this together, to the blessed end."

Beverly tried her hardest to believe his words. It wasn't that she doubted *him*, but her experience told her that it was impossible to hold on to the things one loved. She had expected to love Larry all her life, but fate had gone against her, had robbed her of the one thing she loved most. Now that she dared to love again, would things work out differently? Just because Sheldon loved her and she loved him, would that mean they could spend their lives together? There were so many things that could come between them. What if she had told him about her fear of airplanes before this trip? He would have brought someone else along and never known her feelings. Would they have ever realized their love? Or would their pride have kept them apart all their lives? Beverly just didn't know, and as much as she trusted her feelings now, and his feelings for her, experience had taught her to mistrust the future. She tried not to think this way, but the questions refused to lie unanswered. She sought the answer in Sheldon's eyes, but they were blind with new love. He hadn't been the victim of loss. He was free to trust.

"Now get to work," he said, trying to be stern, "or I'll fire you!" Beverly managed to laugh, to pull her thoughts away from her fears. They kissed again before he left, and she did her best to shift her attention back to the work in front of her.

When Sheldon returned, he looked happier than when he had left her. Beverly had finished her work, packed her things, and arranged to have Sheldon's belongings brought down with hers to the lobby of the hotel.

"You didn't even have a chance to use the swimming pool," Sheldon said regretfully as they left the hotel.

Beverly looked at the pool of dark blue water in a natural setting. It looked more like a pond than a man-made swimming pool, surrounded by palm trees and waterfalls, but she still preferred the ocean. And she was glad for the way they had chosen to spend their time. She could swim in a pool any time.

Sheldon had been busy with the plane in the hours they'd been apart. Now he told her of the hundreds of safety devices that the plane offered, and Beverly did her best to put her trust in the equipment, but all she could think about was how tiny the plane was. In fact, Sheldon had rented a twin-engine plane, large enough to carry six people and their luggage, but it was close to the size of the plane Larry had flown to his death, and nothing Sheldon could say or show her would persuade her to stop worrying. She knew her concern would unsettle him, so she did her best to cover her real feelings.

He helped her aboard, inviting her to sit up front beside

him. "I think the more you see where you're going," he said, "the more you'll feel confident about the flight. You're less likely to be airsick in front, too."

Beverly swallowed the knot in her throat and took the seat beside him, strapping herself to her fate with the double seat belt. She gripped the copilot's steering wheel with all her might as the plane left the ground, and despite her fear she had to acknowledge what a skilled takeoff Sheldon had executed.

Once they were in the air, Sheldon relaxed his attention and invited Beverly to steer the plane, but she declined hastily. Sheldon shrugged and let it pass.

"Quite a view, isn't it?" he said. They were flying over Maui now, the island closest to Hawaii. "There's Haleakala," he said, circling a huge crater.

"Is that a volcano?" Beverly asked, daring a look out the window.

"Yes," Sheldon answered, turning the plane at an angle so they could see inside the mountain. "It's the largest extinct crater in the world," he said. "Something like three thousand feet *deep*!" He laughed huskily. "I'd hate to fall into that one, extinct or not."

"I wonder what it's like inside?"

Sheldon grinned fiendishly. "We could fly closer. . . ." Beverly shook her head so fiercely that he laughed out loud. "I thought not," he said. "As far as I know, it's full of cinder cones, from the volcanic ash that erupted but was never expelled. And a rare herb grows down there."

"I think I would rather cook without it," Beverly said. She looked out the window again, engrossed in the view, forgetting her fear for a moment. "What's that?" she asked, pointing, as they crossed the narrow channel to Hawaii.

Sheldon scanned the edge of the water. "That's a coral reef. The largest reef in the Alenuihaha Channel."

"It's beautiful!" she exclaimed breathlessly. Even from

the air she could see the shadows of blue coral just beneath the water's surface.

"It's a barrier reef," Sheldon went on. "There's a theory that all barrier reefs begin as fringe reefs—that is, they grow around a volcanic island—and when the island begins to sink, the reef becomes a barrier."

"My goodness!" Beverly gasped. "Are these islands sinking?"

Sheldon laughed. "Not that you'd notice. Maybe a couple of inches every thousand years."

"How long do you think it took those little coral to form a colony that size?"

"Millions of years," Sheldon guessed. "Have you ever seen coral close up?" She nodded. "Then you can imagine how long it takes those fragile skeletons to multiply into something that size."

Beverly sighed. They had passed over the reef and were away from land, except for the island ahead of them.

"There's Hawaii," Sheldon pointed out.

"Thank goodness," Beverly said. For the first time on the trip she felt really confident they would survive the journey.

Sheldon landed the plane as expertly as he had taken it from the ground, and in minutes they were at a standstill at the end of a dirt runway. Beverly had expected primitive conditions, but the airstrip was deserted. She accepted Sheldon's hand and jumped onto the airstrip, thankful to have her feet planted on solid ground. "What about the luggage?" she asked, as they walked away from the plane.

"Always worried about our luggage, aren't you?" he teased. "We have to find our car first. No point in carrying it when we don't know where we're going."

Beverly looked down the desolate landing strip, wondering where they would ever find a car. But before she could say anything, she saw a man running toward them.

"Hullo, hullo," he called. He was about five feet tall, and nearly as round. He wore a bright red-flowered shirt and short green pants, and his smile flashed in the bright sunlight. "We are expecting you," he said, taking Sheldon's hand, smiling at Beverly.

"Are you Mr. Kohama?" Sheldon asked.

"I am, I am," the portly man admitted. "And you are Mr. Whitney?" He shook Sheldon's hand again. "Are you Mrs. Whitney?" he asked, smiling broadly at Beverly. She noticed that many of his teeth were missing. Not from all the sugarcane, Beverly hoped.

"This is Miss Milford," Sheldon clarified.

"Ohhhhh," the man said, laughing to himself. "Very well, come with me, please. I have a car for you, and directions to your house. Are you here for long?" he asked.

"All week. The rest of our crew will arrive tomorrow, but they won't be staying overnight," Sheldon said.

Mr. Kohama giggled. "You and the lady have the only house at this end of Hawaii." Suddenly his eyes lit up. "Are you a movie star?" he asked Beverly.

"Oh, no," she said bashfully.

"Miss Milford is my assistant," Sheldon explained.

"I see." He nodded energetically, his wide eyes running up and down Beverly's figure.

Beverly reddened, and Sheldon laughed. "I can see I have to worry about men even here," he whispered, as they followed Mr. Kohama to the tiny office at the end of the airstrip. Beverly tried to hit him with her purse, but she missed.

The car Mr. Kohama presented to them proudly was a '57 Jeep. "Very nice," Sheldon agreed. He and Beverly stifled their laughter until they were out of the office.

They drove the jeep back to the airplane and unloaded their suitcases, secretly delighted by the unexpected adventure. "We don't get much chance to rough it in London,"

Sheldon pointed out, and Beverly agreed that once in a while it was nice to live without the clutter of modern conveniences.

The road to their house was little more than a dirt path, and they had to keep their eyes peeled for tortoises that crossed the road at inopportune moments. They stopped briefly at the filming location, and seeing that it would suit their needs perfectly, they headed down the road to their rental.

"I'm surprised by the terrible roads," Beverly said. "After such beautiful highways in Honolulu."

"Not all the roads are this bad," Sheldon answered. "We're on the east side of the island, because it's the most isolated. But on the west side the roads are more civilized. We could even find a decent hotel in Hilo, I suspect, but to get there we'd have to use roads like this, and I doubt that this jeep would make it. Shall we investigate our rental?"

"Sure. To be truthful, I had expected all of Hawaii, even Honolulu, to look like this."

"About a thousand years ago, it did," Sheldon observed. "Before airplanes brought the tourists."

They reached the rental without mishap, only to find that the house was little more than a shanty. Sheldon used the key, but it was unnecessary. The lock was broken, and Beverly understood why the owner hadn't bothered to repair it. There was nothing inside worth stealing, and no one nearby to try.

"Can you stand it?" Sheldon asked her, after they had explored the rooms.

"I would rather stay here than fly back to Honolulu every night. Can *you* stand it?"

"As long as you're with me, I can live anywhere," he said. "Even here." He kissed her slowly, and as if by magic, the room didn't seem so bad anymore.

"I'll bet if we move some of this furniture around and

sweep the floors, it won't be half bad," Beverly said.

"I'm willing if you are," he answered, looking around.

They worked for an hour, sweeping out the sand and black beetles from the four tiny rooms. There was a pretty tapestry in the closet which they used to cover the holes in the sofa and they found a tablecloth that made the breakfast nook seem cozy. Beverly removed all but two wicker chairs from the kitchen, and Sheldon filled a big jar with lovely flowers he found growing outside the house. The bathroom was hopeless, but at least they had running water. There was one tiny bedroom, and when she saw it Beverly understood Mr. Kohama's insinuating laughter. It was a plain room, but its saving grace was an old-fashioned double bed and an easterly view of the fields.

"Not that I plan to look at anything but you in here," Sheldon said, when she pointed out the benefit of the large windows.

"What will we do for food?" Beverly wondered suddenly.

"That's simple," he told her. "We'll feast on each other!"

"I don't think cannibalism is part of the Hawaiian tradition," she said. "Or is it?"

"Not to worry," he said, "Mr. Kohama said he'd bring groceries by this evening."

"That's very generous of him," Beverly remarked.

"I think he wants another look at you," Sheldon teased. "Shall we explore the island? Did you bring pants to change into?"

"Shorts," she said.

"All the better."

The sun was still high overhead as they walked over the mountainous terrain. After a few miles, the path ended. "I wonder why the road ends?" Beverly said.

"All roads end at Mauna Loa," Sheldon remarked.

"What is Mauna Loa?"

Sheldon pointed at the massive mountain rising in front

of them. It was just one of the steep mountains that they had seen—the entire island was mountainous—but this one disappeared into clouds, and Beverly couldn't see the top of it. "Is it a volcano, too?" she asked.

"It is *the* volcano," he said. "Mauna Loa is the largest active volcano in Hawaii."

"Active?" Beverly gasped. "You mean it might erupt, right now?"

Sheldon laughed. "It might, but there's little chance. The last time it erupted was in 1924. The most we are likely to experience is a tremor. They're quite common, no matter where you are on the island. In fact," he continued, "if the ground trembles, it's supposed to settle the volcano and keep it from erupting."

"That doesn't sound very safe to me. Are you sure we should stay here? Maybe that's why no one lives in this part of the island."

"I don't think we have to worry. We're going to be here such a short time, and if the mountain hasn't bothered to erupt in all these years, it's unlikely that it will while we're here. I haven't done anything to offend the gods, have you?"

"If you think yourself exempt from the god's fury, I guess I'm safe."

"Good. And if the mountain starts smoking, we'll just present you as an offering."

"Sacrifice isn't my line of business. Anyway, I think they only take virgins," she whispered, as if someone were looking over her shoulder.

"Guess that saves you!" he said, ducking to miss her playful fist.

"Let's see if Mr. Kohama has brought us our groceries."

"Good idea. I'm starving! And after supper . . . Got any good ideas?"

Mr. Kohama had delivered three sacks of groceries. He left a message saying he had to go home and that the crew would arrive at nine the next morning. At the bottom of the badly spelled note he scribbled a phone message from the mainland for them. "Your father called."

Sheldon shook his head in dismay. "Something must be wrong," he said. "And I can't even reach him."

"There's no number?" Beverly asked, taking the note from him.

"No. I guess there's nothing I can do about it tonight. Perhaps when the crew arrive they'll have word. No point worrying about it until we know."

"Very strange, though," Beverly admitted, before unpacking the fresh produce from the shopping bag. "My goodness!" she exclaimed. "What I would do for food like this in London!" She lifted a basket of blueberries from one bag. Each one was the size of a marble.

"Looks wonderful," he said, peering inside the bag. "By the way, do you know how to cook?"

"Of course I know how to cook," she told him. "Just tell me what you feel like eating." She glanced around the kitchen. "Anything that can be cooked on one burner and in a foot-square oven."

"Surprise me," Sheldon said. "Like you have ever since we arrived at these enchanted islands." He held her for a minute before she returned her attention to the groceries. She was famished, and it would take her longer than usual to cook in unfamiliar surroundings. Besides, she wanted to prepare something that would dazzle Sheldon's palate.

Sheldon disappeared into the other room. He intended to convert half the living room into their office. She heard him rummaging through his luggage as she unpacked the rest of the food. He reappeared in the kitchen with several bottles of wine. "I secured them from the hotel," he said, smiling.

"You mean you stole them!" she said, examining the labels. He lined the bottles along the counter and returned to his work.

By the time Beverly announced dinner, Sheldon had made considerable progress on his task. When he entered the kitchen he was surprised to find the table elegantly set. A hurricane lamp cast a rosy glow over the steamy kitchen. Beverly handed him a bottle of wine to pour into their glasses; an inch was missing from the top, and she explained that she had used some of the vintage Chablis to cook with.

Proudly Beverly removed the top to the casserole dish, revealing scallops and mushrooms in a white wine sauce over a bed of long-grain brown rice. Then she produced firm stalks of asparagus and an avocado and pineapple salad vinaigrette. Sheldon tasted the scallops before delivering the verdict his eyes had already reached. "You have worked miracles."

Beverly tasted the salad. It was very good, and it didn't hurt that they were hungry. "Wait till you see dessert," she said.

True to her word, when they had finished their meal she produced a blueberry cobbler. She poured thick cream over the hot dessert, and the cream mixed with the blueberries, providing ribbons of purple.

When they had finished the delicious dessert they took their coffee into the living room. Sheldon started a fire. Outside the wind howled; the light drizzle of rain that had begun during dinner had turned into a downpour. Inside they felt protected and safe.

Beverly leaned against Sheldon on the sofa, her feet drawn up beneath her. He wrapped one arm around her waist, and they talked lazily for a while, snug in the funny little house that was their home for the week.

At midnight Sheldon suggested they go to bed, and Beverly didn't need much persuading. Neither of them had had much sleep the night before. The plane ride had taken what little energy she had saved. She was as tired as she was happy, and the morning promised to bring the hardest work of the week. She could tell that Sheldon was tired, too. He had stifled yawns all evening. He had closed his eyes once after dinner, and she had felt him drifting off to sleep before he caught himself.

He smiled languorously as they undressed in the soft glow of the hurricane lamp they had brought from the kitchen. She found her lace nightgown in her suitcase, and for once she felt the occasion suitable for the delicate garment. She slid into bed beside him and snuggled happily into his arms. Turning her face up to his, she offered him a kiss good night. He pressed his lips against hers, and the sleepiness inside her turned to longing. His arms slid over her silky gown, and her skin tingled with excitement from his touch. She returned his kiss with mounting passion as her fingers slid along the row of ivory buttons on his pajama shirt, parting the soft fabric as he parted her lips. In an instant they had forgotten sleep. Quickly he removed her nightgown. Their night clothing lay in a heap on the floor, their exhaustion a thing of the past.

Beverly held Sheldon with all her might. They made love gently, then greedily, as if starved for the food they hadn't tasted since that morning. They tasted the boundaries of their desire rising again and again to their lips. She writhed under his touch, but he held her so tightly that she fought to respond. His hold increased her ecstasy, until she felt the world falling out from beneath her, the law of gravity defied in his expert touch. She ceased to struggle as the last traces of reality fell away. She floated into space, feeling his presence only in a distant hemisphere.

When she returned from flight, she collapsed into his familiar arms, safe in his now gentle embrace. He stroked her face, brushed the hair out of her face, pleased with her journey. "Now sleep," he said softly, bringing the covers up over her satisfied body. In an instant she was sound asleep.

chapter 12

THE SUN FLOODED the bedroom, bringing Beverly from her deep slumber with sudden terror. They had managed to oversleep, and the sun's height convinced her it must be well after ten o'clock.

"Sheldon, love, wake up!" She shook him gently, but he continued to sleep soundly. "Sheldon!" she persisted, shaking him harder.

He woke with a start. "What is it?" he asked instantly.

"We've overslept! Look! The sun is up, and I'm sure we've missed the crew's arrival. They must be waiting for us at the airport now!"

Sheldon seemed less concerned than Beverly, but he dutifully located his watch, then fell back into bed. "It's just after eight," he told her. "We have plenty of time."

"Only eight! But the sun's so high," she said puzzled. "And they'll be here at nine. That's hardly plenty of time."

She was out of bed, racing around the room, trying to find her bathrobe in the tangle of clothing. Sheldon stayed in bed, watching her mad rush. "Slow down," he said patiently. "If we arrive a few minutes late, no one will blame us. After all, we *are* living in total wilderness."

Beverly stopped in her tracks. "What's gotten into you?" she asked. "Since when are you so casual about work? I thought you were the one on this job who watched things like the schedule. Won't our lateness cost us several thousand dollars—and set a casual tone with the rest of the crew?"

"You're probably right," Sheldon agreed, rising out of bed. He shook his head sleepily. "Darling, you'll soon discover that I'm dreadful in the morning. The only way for me to function this early is with loads of black coffee."

"I'll put the water on to boil," she said. "Do you want something quick for breakfast. I can make—"

"Not so fast," he said, taking her into his arms. "What I need more than breakfast is a kiss from you. You're right. We shouldn't be late. But I have a special excuse. Really!"

"And what is that?" she asked. She had been acting like a chicken with her head cut off, and she was embarrassed to have him see her in such a state of distraction. They had a lot to learn about each other's routines, and clearly they moved at different paces in the morning. "What's your good excuse?" she asked again.

"I'm newly in love! Now who's going to begrudge me a few minutes with the woman who captured my heart?" He pressed his warm body against hers and held her tightly until she relaxed in his arms.

For a minute Beverly wondered if he had fallen back asleep, he held her so still, but his hands moved seductively down the back of her robe, and she knew he was far from asleep. "We haven't got time for that!" she insisted, breaking away from his hold. She wanted to fall back into bed with him as much as he did, but she didn't dare act on their impulse.

"All right," he said unhappily. "If I can't have you, I'll have two eggs over easy."

"You're on," she said and ran to the tiny kitchen. She put together a tasty breakfast, surrounding the fried eggs with potatoes, toast, and strawberries that challenged the size of the eggs. She handed Sheldon his first cup of coffee while he shaved, and she lured him out of the bathroom with a second cup when breakfast was ready. She poured the last cup from the pot so he could take it with him in the jeep. By the time they reached the airport, just five minutes before nine, he was awake and ready for the day.

They watched from the jeep as two planes brought the crew into the airport. They would do little shooting that first day, Sheldon explained, but all the crew was necessary to set up for tomorrow. In all, they made a team of fourteen. Two local children would be brought in from Honolulu the next day to pose in the sugarcane field. No one had word from Douglas Whitney.

Everyone was pleasant, and Beverly could tell at once she was going to enjoy working with these people. But there was little time to chat. Later they would get to know each other, when the waiting began, but this first day was crucial to the success of the project, and everyone was busy. Sheldon set the pace, and the others kept up admirably.

His manner was entirely professional. Even in the few moments when they found themselves alone he was all business. At first Beverly felt slighted, but as the day grew more hectic, she saw that there was no room for personal considerations. Not that he was rude to her, but he didn't treat her any differently than he did the others. Once she missed a lighting cue, and she saw the annoyance in his eyes. It hurt much more, to her surprise, than it would have a week ago. She vowed never to slip again.

At the end of the first day Beverly was exhausted. She was quiet on the ride back to the house. Sheldon had been formal with her for such a long time that she wondered if he would continue once they were back in the privacy of their own house. But he surprised her by leaning over to kiss her even before they had left the car. "Thought I had deserted you, didn't you?" he said, and the trembling of her lower lip told him he had guessed correctly. "I'm afraid if I think of you as anything but Miss Milford, my capable assistant, while we're at work, I'll stop working altogether," he explained. Beverly nodded. Sheldon bent to kiss her again. "It's the great danger of working with someone you love," he said. "Most people think it can't work."

"I've never been in love with anyone I've worked with," she said.

"Nor have I," he confided. "In fact, I've never been in love before. It's all very confusing. And I won't survive without your help. Can you help me through this one, Bev? I need you."

She looked at him incredulously. "You've never been in love before?"

"Shameful, isn't it?" he admitted. "A man my age. I should have been in love hundreds of times by now. But it never happened, and it's one of those things you can't make happen. I tried to compensate, but it didn't help. Love has a mind of its own. But now, I can't complain." He took her chin between his thumb and middle finger and lifted her face to his. "You have been worth the wait, Bev. In all my dreams of love, I never imagined I'd feel like this."

Tears flowed from Beverly's eyes. She felt so silly. Here was the man she loved, professing his love for her, and she couldn't stop crying. She started to tell him how much she loved him too, but a strange noise down the road stole her attention.

She looked over her shoulder at the same time Sheldon did. They spotted Mr. Kohama driving madly toward them, his hand waving wildly out the window of his station wagon.

"Telephone! Telephone!" he cried. Beverly and Sheldon hopped out of the jeep to meet him. "Your father! Your father! He is at the mainland. He says you must talk."

"When did he call?" Sheldon asked, trying to keep calm.

"Just now. I came at once. I knew you would want to know."

"May I use your phone?" Sheldon said.

"You can try. The connection I had with the mainland wasn't very clear."

They followed him back to the airstrip in the jeep, the dust from the road stinging Beverly's eyes. "It must be an emergency."

The phone connection was terrible, but Sheldon did reach the hotel. After several minutes of waiting, he heard his father's voice. Beverly could see some of the anxiety disappear from his face.

"Are you all right?" he asked. "What in the world are you doing here?" His voice was agitated. He listened for a minute, then covered the phone to relay the message to Beverly. "He says there's trouble with the sugar contract. He says it's urgent to talk tonight. There's a big meeting scheduled for tomorrow afternoon."

Beverly touched her hand to his sleeve. "You have to go to him, and stay through the meeting and follow-up. I'll be all right."

"Are you sure?" he asked uncertainly. She nodded. He returned to the phone. "Beverly's with me," he explained to his father. He listened again. "No—she'll stay here—I'll explain when I see you. All right, see you soon."

"Is it urgent?" Beverly said when he had hung up.

"Yes. Something about a union strike. And he said if we didn't settle some issues tonight there'd be no shoot for a week or more, and that would ruin our whole schedule. There'd be no point in continuing. Are you sure you won't come with me? I'll be gone a couple of days."

"Positive," she assured him. "Just make sure you come back," she said.

"Just try to keep me away," he said. He glanced at his watch. "Do you want me to drive you back to the house?"

"No. The sooner you go, the sooner you'll be back. Don't worry about me," she added. "I'll ask Mr. Kohama to drive me. That way the car will be here for you when you get back."

"Can I trust you with Mr. Kohama?" he teased her.

"You'll have to hurry home to find out," she retorted. She knew he was stalling. "Go now," she urged.

He hated to go as much as she hated to have him leave, but their love couldn't stand in the way of urgent business. They would be in love for the rest of their lives. There would be many occasions when they would be forced to part. She might as well face that reality now.

"I love you!" she said, and they kissed deeply before he went to the plane. She stayed outside the office until his plane was out of sight. She decided to walk instead of ask for a ride with Mr. Kohama. There was enough daylight still to see her home, and the warm wind felt good on her bare arms.

How she missed Sheldon! Especially because the weather during the two days that had passed without him had been exquisite. Unusually grand even for this unusually grand spot. The skies were bright blue and perfectly clear. Almost abnormally so, Beverly thought as she walked off the beach and back to the little house.

Inside she wrapped herself in Sheldon's light robe—it made her feel as though his arms were around her—and snuggled at the end of the sofa. She idly picked up a book, only to put it down again, preoccupied with Sheldon and the glorious interlude on the island that she wished he'd shared. Her thoughts drifted. The weather had been too perfect, she mused. And then it struck her that it had been *ominously* lovely.

The wind rose while she was eating a light supper in the kitchen. It was blowing harder and accompanied by rain by the time she went back to the sofa to try to read again. At nine o'clock or so she heard a car on the road, and she jumped from her seat on the couch.

Her disappointment at seeing Mr. Kohama was visible. "I was hoping you were Mr. Whitney," she told him, before noticing that the Hawaiian's usual cheer was replaced by a worried look. "Is anything the matter?" she asked suddenly, terrified he had bad news about Sheldon.

"Big trouble, miss," he told her.

"What has happened to Sheldon?" she demanded.

He shook his head. "It isn't Mr. Whitney," he said.

Relief rushed over Beverly. "What's the matter, Mr. Kohama?" she asked. "Please, come in," she said, remembering her manners.

"No time for that," he said hastily. "We must leave at once."

"Leave?" she repeated. "But why?" He was talking so frantically that Beverly couldn't understand him. "Please, tell me what's the matter?"

"Mauna Loa!" he shouted.

"The volcano?" Beverly asked.

"Yes! She is angry. Everyone on this side of the island is leaving!"

"Are you telling me that the mountain is going to erupt?" Beverly asked in horror. "But that's impossible! How do you know?" Could this really be happening?

"A plane radioed me. We must go now."

"But I can't leave here," she told him. "Mr. Whitney is coming back, and he won't know where to find me!"

"But you can't stay here! She is angry! And you will

suffer her wrath if you stay. We must hurry!" he said excitedly.

Beverly didn't know what to do. She couldn't think of leaving the island without telling Sheldon where she was. "Can I reach Honolulu by phone?" she asked.

"All the lines are going dead. Please, miss, you must come with me now! I have others to warn. The plane is going to be very full as it is."

Beverly couldn't think straight. All this was happening too fast. Sheldon was due back any time now—and how would he ever find her? He would have heard about the volcano and be hurrying back to her. He would risk his life trying to save her, and she wouldn't even be here when he arrived! Her heart beat rapidly, but this was no time to fall apart. She had to organize her thinking, and quickly. "I'm staying here," she told Mr. Kohama. "Mr. Whitney is certain to be back as soon as he learns of the danger. I must be here to meet him."

"May the gods protect you, miss," he said, backing out the doorway. "I can't force you to come with me, but I wish I could."

She thought quickly. "Mr. Kohama. When you're out of here safely, will you contact Mr. Whitney? Let him know I'm still here?"

"I will do that," he promised. "Now I must run, or none of us will make it out of here. I hope Mauna Loa changes her mind! If the mirrors crash to the floor, run, as fast as you can, north. Don't wait too long. If you do, Mr. Whitney will find nothing but ash."

Beverly watched as the car drove down the muddy road. The rain was so heavy now that she could see nothing through the curtain of water. She looked at the sky, hoping for some sign of the moon, but the blackness was frightening. The clouds were so low that she felt the weight of them on her shoulders. She closed the door to the gusts of wind and tried to think what she should do.

Things got worse very quickly. Behind the thin walls of the shack, she could feel the elements pounding to get in. If the volcano did erupt, she would have little chance of protecting herself here. "I must be calm," she repeated to herself out loud, and tried to think what Sheldon would do if he were here with her. First of all, he wouldn't panic, she reminded herself. She forced herself to sit down, to clear her head of the hysteria that Mr. Kohama had brought with him. She ran over the facts. Mauna Loa was threatening to erupt. While it was not certain it would blow, Beverly had to be prepared in case it did. She had several choices. She decided to return to the airport for the jeep and bring it back to the house. She would leave Sheldon a note tacked to the wall of the office telling him that she was still at the house. Then she would stay put, no matter how bad the storm got, no matter how much the ground trembled, unless the mirrors fell to the ground. At that point she would load her belongings into the car and drive north as quickly as the old jeep could carry her.

Beverly set about her plan with a calm efficiency. First she changed from Sheldon's robe into shorts and a T-shirt. Since she was going to be drenched anyway, the fewer clothes she wore the less weight she would carry. She kicked off her slippers and left her feet bare. She intended to run to the airport. Shoes would only slow her down.

The roads were entirely mud now, and the rain filled the ruts with puddles so deep that Beverly had to slacken her pace to keep from falling. Why hadn't she thought to ride with Mr. Kohama to the airstrip? Rivulets mixed with the mud, and Beverly had to leap over the streams. Rain coursed down her hair into her face; she brushed the water out of her eyes and kept on running. She was covered in mud, drenched to the bone when she reached the airport at last.

She searched the darkened sky for a sign of Sheldon's

plane, but she saw nothing. The roar of the storm prevented her from hearing any sound of an engine. The airport was deserted. Even the antique plane belonging to Mr. Kohama was no longer there. His car was pulled up to the chain-link fence beside the jeep, and Beverly was relieved to see that the keys to both cars were in the ignition. Good, she thought, when Sheldon arrives he can drive from the airport to the house in Mr. Kohama's car. Hastily Beverly tacked up her note in the office.

The jeep started after a few tries. The floor of the car was filled with rain. Fortunately, it ran off the sides enough to let her drive it. She hugged the side of the road, using the high, matted grass as protection from the deep ruts of mud. Halfway home the car stalled, and Beverly flooded the engine in her fury to start it. She had to force herself to wait a full minute before trying the ignition again; the wait passed like an eternity for her.

By the time she reached the house the wind was so strong she had trouble reaching the door, even though she had parked just a few feet from the entrance to the house. She forced the door shut behind her and leaned against it with all her weight until it latched. It took her a second before she could stop herself from shaking, before she was calm enough to continue her plan for survival.

Most of the papers in the improvised office had blown to the floor. Quickly she gathered them into a bundle, ignoring the ink that ran onto her hands and clothes and mixed with the mud and rain. She found Sheldon's briefcase and crammed the papers inside until it was full. Then she piled more into her suitcase instead of her clothes. They didn't matter. The less she had to carry the better. She looked around the house, wondering what else she should take. She packed Sheldon's possessions and what she could fit of her own into his suitcase. It wouldn't hurt to have them ready to go, even if they decided to leave them behind.

When she had done everything she could think of, she sat back down on the sofa to wait. The clock read half past eleven. Surely Sheldon had learned of the danger she was in and would be back for her any minute. She tried to keep her eyes from the clock. She was certain her constant stare kept the hands from moving. Instead, she focused on the mirror, watching for the slightest tremble. She stood up to look outside at the storm, but she couldn't see anything. She could hardly open the door. It was pointless to search the blackness.

She lifted the heavy suitcase onto the table and opened it. Inside she found a clean pair of shorts and a long-sleeved shirt. She listened at the door for the sound of Sheldon's car, and when she was sure she heard nothing above the storm she hurried to the bathroom to bathe herself in hot water. She didn't bother to wash her hair; instead, she poured cupfuls of water over her head, loosening some of the mud enough so she could pull a brush through the tangles. Without bothering to dry her hair, she twisted it into one plait at the back of her head. At least that would keep the rain from running down the front of her shirt. She stood in the middle of the tub and poured water over the rest of her body. The warm water rinsed the dirt and the chill from her skin. She found a dry towel and rubbed her white skin until it turned pink. When she was thoroughly dry she dressed in the clothes she had set aside and then covered herself again in Sheldon's bathrobe.

The house was unsettlingly quiet. The wind was going down, the rain lightening to a patter on the slanted roof. Beverly saw that the black clouds had passed; a bright moon lit the sky. Relief rushed through her. She had feared the storm would keep Sheldon from landing. She stayed at the window. In the distance, by the light of the moon, she saw a thin stream of smoke puffing above the awesome mountain.

The clock ticked slowly. Beverly forced herself to close her eyes, but she counted the seconds faster than the clock did, and after she had counted sixty ten times, she was dismayed to find that only six minutes had passed. How was she ever going to wait! Where was Sheldon?

Suddenly she thought that he might not return for her. Her thoughts twisted inside her until she couldn't contain them. What if he had decided not to risk returning for her? Sheldon was an important man. His loss would be felt by hundreds. Why should he risk his life for hers? He had *said* he loved her, but would he remember that when faced with his own fatality? He had resisted love all his life. Might he see the burden of it now and be glad to be free of it?

Beverly was working herself into hysteria. She paced the room deliriously, cursing herself for missing her chance to leave the island, for risking her life. A shattering noise spun her around: the mirror had fallen from the wall. Mauna Loa was erupting! She was going to die!

She rushed to the door, pausing only to grab the suitcases she had packed. She threw them into the rear of the jeep, but when she turned the key in the ignition, it wouldn't start. She tried again and again, but the engine wouldn't even turn over. Realizing that the wind and rain had saturated the engine, she gave up trying. She abandoned the car, taking only the briefcase filled with important papers with her.

The wind was so strong that at one point it knocked the briefcase out of Beverly's hand. She decided to leave it behind, afraid it would slow her down.

She couldn't tell how much time had elapsed before she finally reached the deserted airstrip, but she was certain it was hours. Behind her she could hear Mauna Loa's angry threats. The rain was filled with the smell of smoke. Beverly sought refuge from the storm in the office, but she found that the storm had taken the roof off the building. She crouched beneath the counter, which was covered with debris. All her hope was gone. Sheldon would never come for her. Even if he had tried, he couldn't have made it: he would have been here by now! And knowing herself to be responsible for his death, she wished her own.

A blast shook the tiny structure in which Beverly had taken cover. She thought for the last time of her love for Sheldon before her head struck the corner of the counter.

chapter 13

SHE DREAMED SHE was being carried into the clouds. A comfort surrounded her like strong and protective arms. She was no longer afraid. There was nothing to fear at all. Her body felt weightless, her mind relieved of worry. She floated from one billowy cloud to another, and she was returned to a previous time, a time when life had been simpler. She was with Larry again, and that made her very happy—or it should have, but one thought kept the reunion from being perfect, one thought darkened the joyous reconciliation: she would never again hold Sheldon.

Larry appeared to her as he had in the last hours of their life together: kind, caring, loving. He embraced her warmly, and Beverly was joyous to see that he was alive after all, and well. But when he kissed her, she felt nothing of what she had felt when Sheldon had touched her—or even looked at her from across the room.

Larry was taking her back to America, where they would live as they once had, but even this thought was bittersweet. She couldn't bear to be far from Sheldon. What could she do? How could she tell Larry she loved Sheldon, more than she had ever loved Larry? How could she convince him that she had loved him, but her new love for Sheldon was stronger, deeper, more powerful than the bond she had known in marriage? She had no choice but to tell him the truth.

As he approached her, she called out his name, twice, to tell him she could not return to him, that she had to find Sheldon. But he disappeared from her sight as mysteriously as he had appeared. He must have known. He must have seen the truth in her eyes.

She opened her eyes and found Sheldon holding her in his arms, and the last of her fears dissolved. "My darling," she whispered. She was weak, and her voice trembled. "I was trying to find you," she started to tell him.

He looked at her, his dark eyes troubled and unsmiling. "Are you sure it was me you were looking for?" he asked.

Beverly wanted to ask him what he meant, but she felt the pain on the side of her head where she had fallen, and she remembered the storm and the volcano.

Sheldon gathered her into his arms, ignoring her insistence that she could walk. He carried her to the plane and put her down over two seats, fastening her in with a seat belt. "Hang on," he told her sternly. "This is likely to be a rough takeoff."

The plane worked its way down the muddy runway, gaining momentum until it was moving fast enough against the heavy rainfall to leave the ground. The air they traveled through was thick with black ash, and Beverly wondered how Sheldon could see to fly. "Did Mauna Loa erupt?" she asked.

"Look out the window," Sheldon said sharply. Beverly wondered if he resented rescuing her.

She looked out the clouded window. Her head pounded, and she felt a damp stickiness—a trail of blood mixed with the dried mud—down the side of her face. The plane lifted above the clouds with great effort, and Beverly could see that the air was black with smoke. But still she couldn't tell if the volcano had erupted or was just smoking. And she didn't know what had happened after she hit her head. "Are we in danger?" she asked nervously.

"If we make it out of this mess, we'll be mighty lucky. Are you all right?"

"I think so. My eyesight is a little blurred. How did you find me?"

Sheldon shook his head. "I wasn't sure I had," he said. "The airport officials nearly refused to let me fly to Hawaii. They had word that Mauna Loa might erupt any minute. And even if it didn't, the storm was so bad—as you must have known—that they said I'd never make it."

"You sound sorry you did."

Sheldon ignored her remark. "They're thinking of naming this storm, it's such a beaut. It took me four hours to reach the island, and of course no one was here to signal me in. The airstrip was invisible from the air. But I found it somehow. When you're determined enough, anything is possible. Or so I thought," he added grimly.

Beverly was sitting up now. She felt sick to her stomach from the bumpy flight, but she refused to complain. She was thankful to be alive at all; to be with Sheldon was worth any discomfort. She tried to wipe some of the caked dirt from her face but her hands were covered with mud themselves; so were the rest of her clothes. She looked and felt dreadful, but she didn't care about that. What she cared about was the coarse indifference in Sheldon's voice. "Darling, what's the matter?" she asked.

"What a stupid question," he said, his words lashing against her like the back of his hand. "Look around you, if you haven't already. We're likely to die in this mess!"

Beverly looked at him in shock. This didn't sound like the Sheldon she had seen last on the island. Something had happened to change his feelings for her. But what? What had she done? Again she flooded with worry, but she didn't dare ask him now; this was not the time. "Did it take you a long time to find me?" she asked anxiously. She wondered if she had been unconscious for long.

"After I landed, I went to the house," he said. Beverly started to interrupt, but he ignored her. "I saw that the jeep wasn't at the airport, so I assumed you were back at the rental. I tried Kohama's car, but it was too wet to start." Beverly remembered trying to start the jeep. The details of the storm were beginning to come back to her. She watched the storm from the window of the plane, waiting for Sheldon to continue.

"I ran to the house as fast as I could. I've never seen mud so deep. I searched the house, but you weren't there. I could hear Mauna Loa in the background, threatening to blow any minute, so I headed back for the airstrip, looking along the side of the road for you. It was still dark out, but close to morning, I figured. I was beginning to think you had left the island, that Kohama had forced you to come with him."

"He tried," she interjected.

"I was pretty sure that you wouldn't have left of your own free will. Knowing how stubborn you can be," he added. "I had thought you would stay put, to wait for me to come back for you. That's why I didn't listen to those guys at the airport."

"Mr. Kohama tried to convince me I'd die, but I had to stay. I kept thinking, what if Sheldon returns and I'm not here? He'll have made the trip for nothing."

Sheldon glared at her. "What *if* Sheldon returns...? Didn't you *know* I would be back?" he demanded. "Didn't you trust that I would have come back for you?"

"I knew you would if you *could*," she said apologetically, afraid of his wrath. "But so much time passed, I thought..."

"What did you think?" he asked snidely.

"I thought maybe you hadn't been able to leave Honolulu. Or—"

"Or what?"

"Or that you decided that the risk was too great," she admitted, biting her lip in shame.

"I see," he said. "I'm glad one of us had more faith in the value of our 'love'." He placed a strange emphasis on the word love, as if scorning it. "Anyway," he said, leaving her to ponder his meaning, "I searched for you along the road back to the airport. I saw the briefcase about halfway down the road, and I had to laugh. At that point I figured you were safe. It must have broken your heart to leave the contracts behind in the mud."

Beverly listened to him, a feeling of unhappiness overshadowing the joy she had first felt at seeing him. He had obviously decided his love for her had been a mistake, and she almost wished he had left her to die rather than live with this discovery. At least with her death she would have had his love, his concern. Now everything she had to live for was slipping out of her grasp, and she didn't know what she could do to prevent it.

The wind was lifting the plane out of Sheldon's control. The sky was so black that she couldn't see out the window; surely Sheldon couldn't do more than guess the direction he was flying in. "Are we going to make it?" she asked, not really caring anymore.

"Not if my luck continues the way it has tonight," he growled. He grabbed the controls and brought the plane to a higher altitude. For an instant the plane cleared the blackness, and Beverly could see a stretch of blue sky—the beginning of daylight, a renewal of hope. Just as quickly as it had appeared, however, the blue blackened with ash, and Sheldon flew on into the darkness. "My guess is that if we can make it out of this line of ash, all we'll have to contend with is the storm."

"What about landing the plane on one of those little

islands we passed flying to Hawaii?" Beverly suggested. "Until the storm passes."

Sheldon took his eyes from the blackened mass in front of him. "I think that might be worth a try," he conceded. "The only trouble is finding a place to land."

"Do you remember that stretch of land right before we saw the coral reefs?" Beverly recalled. Sheldon opened his eyes wide, remembering having seen a field a few moments before Beverly pointed out the blue coral.

"The only trick would be missing the reef," he said. "But our chances are better with that than fighting this storm. We've passed most of the volcanic ash, but we're nearly out of fuel. You're going to have to guide me," he told her. "Take the copilot's seat. I hope you have a better line of vision out your window than I have straight ahead."

Beverly moved to sit beside him. "All I can see is water," she said. "Wait—can you fly a little lower?" Sheldon brought the plane closer to the water, and she could see the white caps from her side of the plane. "That's close enough." Sheldon leveled the plane just in time to miss the peaks of the waves. "There!" Beverly exclaimed excitedly. "I see the coral reef. Lift up!"

Sheldon raised the plane just in time to miss scraping the bottom of the aircraft on the sharp rise of coral. "The field should be just past here," he assured her, but the quake in his voice told Beverly just how near a miss they had experienced. A sharp piece of coral could have ripped the bottom of the plane like scissors cutting through paper. "That is, if we're at the right coral reef. It's hard to be sure, there are so many around here."

"This is the right one," Beverly assured him. "I remember seeing a treelike mass of coral, and I just spotted it again. I'm sure this is it." Sheldon looked impressed in spite of himself. "And I think," she continued, watching the reef below, "if I remember correctly, that the field was further north."

"I think you're right," he said and maneuvered the plane to the left.

They were beyond the danger of Mauna Loa now, but neither of them thought it wise to tempt their fate with congratulations. The storm was more wild than ever, and Beverly realized, for the first time, just how dangerous it was in its own right. "Is that it?" she asked, seeing a patch of even ground amid the mountainous terrain of Maui's coastline.

Sheldon strained to see through the rain. "I can't say for sure. I was thinking about other things on the way over here. It might well be."

He brought the plane lower, and Beverly could hear the landing gears lock into place. "Just in case," he told her. "You'd better fasten that other seat belt."

The wheels of the plane touched ground, then bounced back up into the air, jolting them in their seats. Sheldon tried again to calm the plane into landing, slowing the landing by breaking the engine's speed. Again and again the wheels skidded along the field, and finally Sheldon held the plane on the ground for more than an instant, but the wind was against them and the gusts forced the plane up again. Sheldon had no choice but to bring the plane back into flight. "We'll have to approach it from the other direction," he explained.

"But this is the field?"

"It's the field, all right," he said, his teeth clenched. "But it's a lot shorter than I remembered, and not as smooth close up as it looks from the air."

"But we'll make it?" Beverly asked hopefully.

"I'll give it everything I've got," he said, turning the plane around.

"Then we're bound to make it," she said under her breath.

He approached the field from the opposite direction. The wind played with the tiny plane as if it were a paper kite. Sheldon touched ground once, too hard, and Beverly hit her chin against the window ledge. The second time he touched the wheels to the ground they held.

It took all his force, but he kept the plane steady on the ground and slowed it to a halt before the makeshift runway ended. They bounced along through an uneven field of harvested plants, the stocks breaking angrily against the plane, until a rock caught the wheel and spun them around.

Sheldon released a deep breath when the plane came to a standstill. Beverly managed to swallow, but her mouth was dry. She looked over at Sheldon, but he stared straight ahead. The nose of the plane was lodged in a pile of weather-beaten lumber. Outside the storm continued to rage. "I think the plane is ruined," Sheldon remarked in a defeated voice. They were a long way from safety.

"At least we're alive," Beverly whispered. "Thank heaven for your skill as a pilot."

Sheldon looked at her coldly. "Yes. At least we're alive." He lifted himself out of the pilot's seat and went over to the rear of the plane.

Beverly followed him at once. "Sheldon!" she called. "Tell me what I've done! You act as if you're sorry that you came back for me." He didn't say anything but closed his eyes, as if to shield them from her. "Are you?" she demanded. "But why!"

"I'm not sorry you're alive, if that's what you mean," he said, but his voice was void of feeling.

"Then what's wrong?" she insisted. She reached over to touch his arm, but he recoiled from her as if he had been struck. "You act as if you can't stand being near me."

"Looks like I don't have a choice, do I?" He glared at her. "We don't stand a chance of getting out of here until the storm is over. And even then I'm not sure I can make this thing fly again."

"Is that what's bothering you?" she persisted. He shook his head slowly. "Then tell me. You owe me that much."

"You've been lying to me, that's all. And I've been a fool to believe you. I even risked my life to come back to you, when the entire island of Oahu was saying it was insane to try. I should have listened."

"Then you are sorry you came back."

"I would rather have remembered you as I left you," he said. "I would rather have had the lie of your 'love' for me intact. It pains me to learn differently, if you must know."

"What in the world are you talking about? Do you think I don't love you? How can you possibly—"

"What I *want* to think and what I *do* think are two different things," he said slowly, as if talking to a child. "And if I listen to you, you'll try to convince me that you really do care, and because I want to believe you I will. But you don't."

"I do!"

"No, Beverly, you don't. And the sooner you admit that you've been using me the better for both of us. We're both reasonable adults. We can face the truth, even if it stings a bit."

"When you left you believed I loved you. I haven't changed my feelings. If one of us has, it's you. If you want out of this affair I won't keep you, but don't blame it on me! The least you can do is explain yourself," she demanded. "If you want to know what I think, I think this flight has jarred you in the head!"

Sheldon shook his head sadly. "No, luv. The flight hasn't jarred me, but the storm jarred you. You were asking how I found you. Well, I never finished telling you. When I got back to the airport and I still hadn't found you, I was sure you had left with Kohama, until I heard you calling. The storm was so loud, and your voice was so soft, I almost didn't hear you. But in the short time we've been together I've come to know your sweet voice very well. Only this time what threw me was that you were calling for Larry!"

He glared at her, as if he had explained everything. "It was all I could do to go to you anyway."

"But I was unconscious," she protested. "Don't you see—"

"That's just it," he interrupted, his case proven beyond a doubt. "You were calling for him out of your unconscious. You don't even know that you still love him. How can you love me when your heart is calling out for him?"

The details of the dream were coming back to her. She remembered why she had been calling for Larry, but she didn't see how she could explain it coherently to Sheldon. Still, she had to try. "I know this will sound crazy," she started, and Sheldon's skeptical look almost defied her to go on. "I dreamed that Larry had come back for me. We were going to live the life we had imagined we would."

"Please, spare me the—"

"No!" she said harshly. "You listen to me! You're acting like a wounded lion, and you have to see that it's just a thorn in your paw." Sheldon frowned, but he waited for her to go on. "As I said, Larry had come back to find me. I was happy to see him, of course, except for one thing."

"And what was that?" Sheldon asked bitterly.

"That if I went with him, I couldn't be with you," she said tranquilly.

"Do you expect me to—"

"I was calling out to him, to explain that I had to leave him. You see, I had no choice. I love *you*, you idiot."

"Do you mean to tell me you don't love him?"

"No," she said. "I didn't say that."

A look of satisfaction appeared on his face. "I thought so."

She ignored him. "No," she repeated emphatically. "I will always love Larry. He was my childhood sweetheart. I married him intending to spend my whole life with him, and I would have if he hadn't been killed. But since then

I met you. And in spite of all my attempts to not love you, I did and I do." She paused; Sheldon was listening to her now. "I'll always love Larry. He was good to me, like a brother. But you are my real love. You are the first man I have loved passionately. Larry didn't know me the way you do. Larry knew me as a girl. I love you as a woman."

Sheldon reached out and drew Beverly into his embrace, holding her close, his chest pounding wildly against her breast. "I love you, Bev. I was scared to death that you were . . . And then when I found you and you were calling for . . . I didn't know which was worse. I thought I had lost you just when I had found you."

"You'll never have to worry about losing me. As long as you want me, I'll be yours."

"Forever?" he asked.

"As long as you want me."

"Well then, let's get out of this place," he said with renewed vitality. He pointed out the window, and Beverly saw that the storm had subsided into a light rain. She started to open the door, but he stopped her. "On one condition," he stated. "The only motivation I have for going back is to marry you. Will you marry me?"

"If there were a captain on board, I'd marry you this minute," she chimed happily. He kissed her slowly, their breaths intermingling like their hopes.

"Then I'd never care about getting out of here," he said and pressed his mouth against hers again. They kissed deeply, joyfully.

chapter 14

THE PLANE WAS damaged, but not irreparably.

It took several hours before they were ready to try to take off and several more hours before they were successful. Once in the air, however, there was nothing that could stop them. Sheldon radioed the Honolulu airport for assistance in landing. One of the wheels had broken loose, and it was going to be a tricky landing.

They could hear cheers from the control tower over the radio. The airport crew had given up hope of ever hearing from him again. The plane had been spotted going down near the reefs. The chief of control at the tower assured them they would be ready to bring them in safely. "But hold on a minute," he said through static. "There's someone here who insists on talking to you."

"Sheldon, Sheldon! Thank goodness you're all right," Sheldon's father shouted. "Is—is Beverly with you?"

"Right by my side, Dad," he assured him. "I wouldn't have come home without her."

"Don't take any side trips," Douglas Whitney said, chuckling. "You have a group of concerned friends waiting to greet you."

"Friends?" Beverly asked.

"Who's there?" Sheldon asked happily.

"You just hurry back and see for yourself," a sassy French voice replied. "We have missed you, Sheldon. And we love you, Beverly."

"Is that Celeste?" Beverly asked, grabbing the control from Sheldon.

"Oui," the voice answered. "And you must fly as fast as you can. I have waited to see you too long already," she said. She was crying unashamedly.

Sheldon took the control back from Beverly. "We're on our way. Have the cake ready for our landing. Over and out."

"The cake?" Beverly said.

"You did say you'd marry me, didn't you?" Sheldon asked. "Because if you've changed your mind, I'm taking you back to Mauna Loa!"

"I will, I will!" Beverly protested. "But—"

"And we have our witnesses waiting. We can't disappoint them." He grinned.

Beverly giggled. "Can I at least wash the mud off my face first?"

"If you insist. But only if you promise to hurry."

The landing was difficult. For a moment Beverly's fear returned, especially when she spotted two fire trucks and an ambulance below.

The ambulance reached them at the end of the runway, where the plane came to a safe, if graceless, landing. Celeste was the first to climb out, followed by Douglas Whitney. Celeste embraced Beverly, while Douglas threw convention aside and hugged his son; then Celeste smothered Sheldon with hundreds of kisses and endearments while Douglas held Beverly.

The red tape was held to a minimum, and soon they were

in the limousine on their way to the hotel.

"What would you like most when we get there?" Sheldon asked Beverly when the hotel was in sight.

"If I say a bath, will you think I don't want you most?"

"I'd be happier if you asked for a shower," he confessed. "Less time for you to be out of my sight."

Celeste laughed at their exchange. "You two have no imagination," she chided. "Do you not think of showering together?" Her eyes danced, and Douglas played the embarrassed father by clearing his throat noisily.

"Do you think there would be enough room in the bathroom for us both with all this mud?" Beverly asked.

"I'm willing to find out," Sheldon retorted.

"We'll have to have someone look at that bump on your head," Douglas remarked. "I can see that you two lovebirds can't wait to be alone, but I'm afraid there are others waiting to greet you."

"Who?" Beverly asked quickly. She turned to Celeste. "Did André come with you?"

"But of course!"

The car pulled into the driveway in front of the hotel, and Beverly spotted André standing out in front. At his side stood Jancie, and beside her, Julian. "Oh, Sheldon!" she cried happily. "Did you know?"

"I had an idea," he said, chuckling. "I wanted to meet Jancie, and I figured this was the only way."

"He phoned us all," Celeste confessed. "But when we arrived we didn't know if it was for the wedding or the..." She didn't continue. There had been no telling if either Sheldon or Beverly would return to Honolulu alive.

Beverly hugged Jancie gleefully, then Julian, and finally André. When she stepped back to look at them all, still not believing her good fortune, she saw they were all covered in dirt from her embrace. But no one cared. All they cared about was her safety, and Sheldon's.

"What are you doing in Honolulu?" Beverly asked Jancie on the way into the hotel.

"It's as good a place as any for a honeymoon, don't you think?" she said coyly.

"You don't mean!!"

"I do! We would have waited for your return to England, but Julian got a little impatient. He said he had been waiting long enough." Julian smiled modestly at her side. They looked so content together. They had obviously made the right decision. "We had a quiet ceremony in London, with just Julian's mum and dad. Then Sheldon rang us."

"So you see," Julian chimed in. "The honeymoon has yet to begin."

Everyone in the elevator car laughed, and Julian blushed deeply.

When the elevator stopped they all got out at the same time. "I've asked for the honeymoon suite," Sheldon said, walking past the room in which he and Beverly had first consummated their love. "If you think I'm going to be outdone by your two friends, you're wrong. I've waited long enough, too!" He opened the door to their new suite of rooms. The sitting room was plush white, with silver and blue furnishings. The door to what Beverly assumed to be the bedroom was shut. The group settled into the modern furnishings, but Beverly didn't want to sit. She was too dirty and too excited.

"But darling, won't it be bad luck for us to stay in the honeymoon suite without being married?"

"First of all," he said. "I think we have had our dose of bad luck for this lifetime. And secondly, if you'll hurry up and finish your bath, we'll correct our unmarried state."

"But..." Her mind was whirling. So much had happened. "But I haven't any clothes to wear. And I can't be married in these things!" she insisted. Everyone looked at her mud-covered shorts and blouse.

Her friends laughed at her worry. Celeste clapped her hands together excitedly, but André was the first to speak. "I do not want to be accused of reading your minds, but I did bring a pretty white dress for you. You will find it hanging in your dressing-room wardrobe."

"Just wait till you see the beautiful gown he created for your wedding!" Celeste announced proudly. "But do not look until after you have showered!"

"You will find a few other things to go with your dress," André said, gesturing past the closed door.

"And if you need to borrow anything from me," Jancie offered, "I have nearly everything I own with me." She looked so happy seated beside Julian.

"Now we must clear out," Douglas Whitney prompted. "And let these two clean up."

"What time do we cut the cake?" Celeste asked eagerly.

"How long do you think it will take you to get out of that mud?" Sheldon asked Beverly.

She looked at him distractedly, then around at the smiling group. She could hardly believe that all this was happening. She was to be married to Sheldon Whitney! "I better have at least an hour," she said, touching her hair.

Sheldon laughed. "I'll need a bit longer than that," he admitted. "Let's meet in your suite, Father, in a couple of hours. All right?" Everyone nodded agreeably. "I'm going to need something to wear too. André, I assume you'll want to help Beverly with her dress, but would you first help me find a decent suit of clothes?" André nodded. "Julian, as a newly married man, I would appreciate any help you could offer me on the kind of ring a girl might like." Julian beamed at being asked his advice. "I assume you women will want to help Beverly dress, too?" Both women nodded happily. "Father, would you make sure all the details for the wedding are set?"

"Right-o!" the old man said. "Now let's get this show on the road. Before another storm finds us!" The group filed out of the hotel suite, promising to be back shortly.

At last Beverly and Sheldon were alone. All of the confidence with which Sheldon had orchestrated their wedding plans now dissolved. He glanced at Beverly. She looked back up at him, waiting. "Are you sure you want this, Bev? You look uncertain," he said, taking both her small shoulders into his strong hands. "We don't have to go through with anything you don't want. I had to act decisive for them, you know, so that they wouldn't continue to worry. I can imagine how hard it was on them to wait, not knowing if they were going to celebrate with us or bury us." She shook her head sadly at the sorrow she had caused her friends. "But if you aren't ready, or if you want to change your mind," he said quietly, "they'll understand."

"Would you?" she asked placidly.

Sheldon swallowed hard. "I—I—if you decided you didn't want to marry me, I would assume you had a good reason. I wouldn't like it, whatever it was, but I'd respect your right to make it. Is it Larry?" he added feebly.

"No, it isn't Larry. What I told you is true. I'll always love him, but I want to spend my life with you. It's you I want to hold night after night, to wake up to, to sleep beside."

"Then why? I don't understand. Is there some other reason?"

"Yes," she told him evenly. "I have this job I adore, and everyone knows you can't work with someone you love."

"You mean you want to keep working with me, and because of that you won't marry me?"

"Unless you have a better idea of how I can fill my time," she said. He stared at her. "Any ideas?"

"I must confess you have me bewildered. Unless..." his voice trailed off as he suddenly remembered what Beverly had said she wanted to do most in the world. "Maybe I could interest you in another challenging job."

"Would it involve any flying?" she asked. She could tell by his eyes that he had remembered the one thing that could take the place of her present job.

"There would be a certain amount of 'flying,' but only until we were sure the 'employment' was secured."

"How soon would this 'job' be available?"

"We could begin 'interviewing' immediately. To give this 'job' the right beginning, I think we should make legal our agreement."

"I accept, Mr. Whitney. I must say you propose the best employment opportunities around. This child of ours is likely to be Whitney-Forbes's finest product to date!"

"Leave Forbes out of this, and you've got yourself a job, Miss Milford. Now let's wash that mud off you, and I'll make you an honest woman. No—I take that back—you are an honest woman. All I can do is make you mine."

"No," she said. "You can't make me that." He looked at her, bewildered. "I'm yours already!" she exclaimed joyfully. "And I will be forever!"

He lifted her off her feet and held her tightly in his arms. "Come with me," he said, carrying her into the other room.

"Now this is the kind of flying I could learn to love!" she said before the door swung shut behind them.

AN ARTFUL LADY #6
by Sabina Clark
Widowed in scandal, and as exquisite as the London society dazzlers whose portraits she paints, the mysterious Sara Roche presents a fascinating challenge to the rake who thought he was too cynical for love.

EMERALD BAY #7
by Winter Ames
By the gem-like waters of Lake Tahoe, Nan Gilliam, just divorced and still hurting, tries to meet the demands of a famous film producer while fighting an overwhelming attraction to the resort's most powerful tycoon.

RAPTURE REGAINED #8
by Serena Alexander
The irresistible pulls of exotic Africa House...and the even more exotic man who'd loved and left her six years before...threaten renewed heartbreak for Cathy Dawson when she comes back from America to the beautiful, magical country of Malawi.

THE CAUTIOUS HEART #9
by Philippa Heywood
Eleanor Portland, a still flawless beauty once touched by scandal, dares a return to London society—to Viscount Lennox, her old tormenting love, and to Lord Merriot, a new, fascinating threat to her reputation...and her heart.

ALOHA, YESTERDAY #10
by Meredith Kingston
Young, voluptuous Christine Hanover scarcely notices the sundrenched, shimmering beauty of her Hawaiian home...until virile, sensitive Nick Carruthers storms into her life.

MOONFIRE MELODY #11
by Lily Bradford
Stranded in the mountain wilderness of Utah, lovely spirited Valerie Sheppard can't wait to get back to New York and her fiance—and away from the seductive haunting tunes played by that infuriating man McKenzie.

MEETING WITH THE PAST #12
by Caroline Halter
Portugal—charming cities, quaint towns, and the thrilling start of a new career, new life for lovely Alex Jameson after the sad collapse of her marriage. Then her mysterious employer arrives in Lisbon to jeopardize her hopes... and her emotions.

Second Chance at Love ™

WINDS OF MORNING #13
by Laurie Marath
Lovely Jennifer Logan believed she'd left troubled love far behind when she came to Glengarriff, the small village on Ireland's coast...until she met the most difficult, haunted—and completely wonderful—man in the world!

HARD TO HANDLE #14
by Susanna Collins
The Belgian aristocrat is a supremely talented equestrian and trainer, an arrestingly handsome, passionate man. But the moment beautiful, widowed Ariane Charles sees him, she knows he's more dangerous to her than an untamed stallion.

BELOVED PIRATE #15
by Margie Michaels
The crystal waters of the Bahamas hold the treasure-find of a lifetime...and the test of a lifetime, too, for stunning Lorelei Averill as she meets again the man she'd once loved too well.

PASSION'S FLIGHT #16
by Marilyn Mathieu
Cool and elusive as a spring mist, Beverly Milford resists the devastating charm of the celebrated lover who is her boss. In Paris, then Hawaii, her defenses erode and the lovely widow is in emotional peril...again.

HEART OF THE GLEN #17
by Lily Bradford
Roaming the byways of Scotland, scouting for antiques, Julie Boland encounters sharp-tongued Ian Fraser. His attractions are enormous, his emotions seem as fickle as her faithless ex-husband's... can the handsome laird erase Julie's bitter memories?

BIRD OF PARADISE #18
by Winter Ames
Brilliant as she is beautiful, Sara Mancini continues her agricultural experiments on Eric Thoreson's Panamanian coffee plantation—despite the interference of her late husband's family...of the tempestuous Rima...and of her irresistible employer.

**TO GET THESE BREATHLESS TALES
OF LOVERS LOST AND FOUND
PLEASE USE THE ORDER FORM
ON THE FOLLOWING PAGE**

Second Chance at Love™

Jove's Thrilling New Romance Line